CHRISTMAS SCANDALS

BOOKS 1-3

SUZANNA MEDEIROS

ZINIA PRESS

A VISCOUNT FOR CHRISTMAS

CHRISTMAS SCANDALS

BOOK 1

ABOUT THIS BOOK

An unexpected Christmas gift…

When Viscount Isaac Thornton returns home for his mother's annual Christmas gathering, the last thing he expects to find is a beautiful woman sleeping in his bed. But Celia isn't yet another woman trying to trap him into marriage. She's his younger sister's best friend and now she's all grown up.

Celia Rowland outgrew the infatuation she had for Thornton years ago. When a misunderstanding means she's been compromised, her mother insists they get married.

One house party and two people trying to escape a forced wedding who just might get the Christmas gift they didn't know they wanted.

❄

To learn about Suzanna Medeiros's future books, you can sign up for her newsletter at suzannamedeiros.com/newsletter.

*In these very difficult times, I hope we can all manage to find
a little joy.*

- Suzanna -

CHAPTER 1

December 1816

IT WAS PAST MIDNIGHT when Viscount Isaac Thornton reached his estate in Surrey. He'd been on horseback for several hours. Normally the ride wasn't a difficult one, but with the cold temperatures, he'd needed to stop frequently to change horses.

Filled with a bone-deep fatigue that emphasized the unwelcome fact he'd recently passed his thirtieth birthday, all he wanted to do was sleep. He wasn't looking forward to the next week. His mother's yearly Christmas party would be yet another opportunity for her to remind him he needed to settle down and produce an heir. He couldn't avoid his mother's matchmaking altogether, but he could limit the duration of his suffering. Which was why he'd originally planned to arrive the day before Christmas and depart again the day after the holiday.

She'd successfully thwarted those plans with the greatest weapon in her arsenal—guilt. He'd received her letter that afternoon. In it, she told him how much she looked forward to spending quality time with him. She'd gone on to inform him that his two younger sisters, who lived in the north of England, wouldn't be attending because the roads were impassable after a heavy snowfall that hadn't reached Surrey. To alleviate what he knew would be her very real disappointment, he'd changed his plans and set out to join her when her house party would still be in full swing.

If he were being honest with himself, London had become tedious of late, especially after his friends and most of his acquaintances quit town and headed to their own estates for the holiday season. His mother's letter was a convenient excuse to return home earlier than planned.

He apologized to the sleepy groom who greeted him moments after he reached the stables. He was relieved to discover the manor was quiet as he made his way to the front door on foot. Perhaps his mother hadn't invited that many people this year.

But even as the thought occurred to him, he knew it was a futile wish. Christmas was his mother's favorite time of the year, and she was known for her winter house parties. This year wouldn't be any different.

He was surprised when the front door was opened by Saunders, their butler, and not a footman. He'd hoped to surprise his mother, but apparently she knew him too well. She'd expected him to set out for Surrey after receiving her letter.

He greeted the older man and handed him his hat and greatcoat, barely taking in the evergreen boughs and festive decorations that tastefully highlighted the fact the festive season was upon them. He'd started toward the stairs when Saunders coughed discreetly.

Thornton turned to face him.

"Your mother wishes to speak with you, my lord."

Thornton frowned. No doubt she wanted to tell him who she'd invited and why he should pay particular attention to each one of them. He'd just arrived, and already the matchmaking had begun.

He nodded. "I'll speak to her in the morning."

"She insisted—"

Thornton wouldn't take his annoyance out on this man whom he'd known since he was a child. Saunders was merely carrying out Lady Thornton's instructions.

"I already know what she wants to speak to me about."

"But—"

"Good night, Saunders. I'll speak to my mother first thing in the morning. And get some rest yourself." The man had no doubt been awake since dawn.

Before Saunders could say another word, Thornton turned and made his way upstairs.

He didn't ring for his valet when he reached his bedroom, too tired to care about the lecture the man would deliver tomorrow as he tossed his clothes onto a chair.

It was dark, but he didn't need to light a candle. He made his way to the bed and slid under the covers. His eyes were closing when a small movement on the other side of the bed chased away his fatigue.

He was imagining things. Or, more likely, he'd already fallen asleep and was dreaming. Still, he was wide awake now. He rolled over and narrowed his gaze on the other side of the bed, where he could see a small bundle wrapped in his blankets.

In retrospect, he should have sprung from the bed and thrown on his clothes. But he didn't really expect to find anything, and so he pulled back the bedsheets. It took his befuddled senses several seconds to process the fact he wasn't alone.

Someone was already asleep in his bed—a woman, to be precise. She lay with her back to him, and he could only stare at her for what felt like the longest minute of his life.

His fumbling in the dark hadn't caused her to move, so she must be asleep. His gaze took in the long golden hair that covered most of her back. Unbound, which surprised him. Unable to stop himself, he gazed down to where her hair ended just above the curve of her hip, which was covered in a white nightgown. The blankets covered the rest of her, and he resisted the temptation to drag them down even farther.

Casting aside the temptation to see whether she would be well endowed, he shifted onto his back and slung a hand over his eyes. He doubted very much that his mother had arranged this woman as a welcome-home present for him. She'd probably wanted to warn him that she had given away his room to another guest.

Which meant he had to dress again and find a servant to lead him to a room that was unoccupied.

He rose to a seating position with a muffled groan. He thought he'd been quiet, but the shifting of his weight must have woken the woman, because she rolled onto her back. Her eyes blinked open, and she let out a sleepy yawn. And then a scream.

That should have had him moving with alacrity, gathering up his clothes and escaping into the dressing room. But his brief glimpse at her form before she'd pulled up the bedcovers caused him to freeze. In the dim light, he could see that she was, indeed, well endowed.

Why did these things never happen to him under better circumstances? For it was clear now that he wasn't dreaming. If he were, she would have beckoned him to her with open arms. Instead, the woman in his bed had gathered up the blankets and held them to her breast like a shield.

"What are you doing here? You must leave at once!"

Yes, this wasn't a dream. "This is my bedroom."

Her mouth gaped open before she closed it with a snap. "You're not suggesting…" She took a deep breath and began again. "We can sort out this mess tomorrow morning. But a gentleman would leave without question and find another bedroom."

He couldn't resist teasing her. "Perhaps I'm not a gentleman."

She sputtered, speechless. Taking pity on her, he slipped from the bed with a soft curse.

"I don't know why you're upset. I'm the injured party here."

Something about the prim tone of her voice seemed familiar. He strode to the window and drew back the curtains to let in some of the moonlight. Then he returned to the bed—the side the woman occupied—and leaned forward to examine her. She leaned back with a squawk.

His eyes roamed over her face. Blond hair, blue eyes… she could have been anyone. But then he saw the small mole at the corner of her right eye.

"Celia Rowland?"

She huffed out an impatient breath. "That's Miss Rowland to you, my lord. Now will you please leave?"

He had to give her credit. Another woman might have given in to a fit of vapors at finding a man in her bed, but not Celia. He remembered her only as his youngest sister's friend. She'd been pretty, and he remembered finding her sweet, but she'd also been much too young for him the last time he'd seen her. He couldn't deny that she'd grown into a beautiful young woman.

He didn't miss the way her gaze dipped to his bare chest and couldn't hold back his smirk. "Like what you see?"

Her eyes met his again. "I was merely—"

"Admiring my fine form? Wondering if you'd asked me to leave too soon?"

She let out an impatient huff. "Is it your intention to compromise me?"

And that's when the reality of the situation settled into place. His understanding came too late, however, because the bedroom door was thrown open.

CHAPTER 2

THE DOWAGER VISCOUNTESS THORNTON had shown Celia to her son's room a few hours earlier, telling her that something was amiss with the room she was supposed to occupy. She'd assured Celia that he wasn't expected back that night, so it had come as a shock to find herself sharing a bed with the almost-naked viscount.

The man for whom she'd had a *tendre* when she was still a silly young girl who only interacted with him on rare occasions when she was visiting his sisters. Despite his well-known penchant for teasing, she knew Thornton would never harm her. He would dress and then find somewhere else to sleep that night.

But even more shocking than her unexpected

awakening was the sound of the bedroom door being thrown open with such force it bounced off the wall with a loud boom. And of course the person standing in the doorway would be her mother. How did she even know Celia had switched rooms for the night? Mama had already retired when Thornton's mother escorted her to this room.

Her mother held an oil lamp aloft as she stepped into the room, her eyes and mouth open in outrage. But then her mouth snapped close, and the glint in her eye made it clear she was delighted to catch them in such a compromising position. Celia in her nightgown, clutching a blanket to her breast, and Thornton standing in only his smallclothes, uncaring that his chest was bare.

Heavens, what a chest it was. He'd caught her staring, but could he blame her?

"What is the meaning of this?"

Celia wanted to roll her eyes at her mother's theatrics, but the situation was dire. "Nothing happened, Mama. It was a misunderstanding."

Thornton ignored her mother's theatrics. Instead, he walked over to the clothing he'd deposited on a chair, acting for all the world as though he were fully dressed, and collected the garments.

"If you'll excuse me for a moment," he said to her mother with a small bow. He moved off to the dressing room, closing the door behind him.

Her mother, however, seemed content to wake the entire house. Celia rose from the bed, hoping to drag her mother into the bedroom and close the door.

She was too late. She'd only managed to take a step in her mother's direction when others began to move into place behind her mother. She reached for her dressing gown, donning it with haste, as guests began doing everything in their power to peer over her mother's shoulders.

"Mama—"

"This is enough. There is nothing to see here. Please go to bed."

The dowager viscountess pushed her way past the growing crowd. Celia's mother resisted but finally allowed Lady Thornton to drag her into the bedroom and close the door behind her. Murmured voices of protest could be heard, dimming after a minute had passed. Celia had no doubt that an army of footmen was leading the guests back to their rooms. They never would have left otherwise.

Lady Thornton frowned at Celia's mother. "For heaven's sake, please lower your voice." She turned to Celia. "Can you explain what is happening here and why your mother sought to raise the entire household?"

Thornton chose that moment to step out of the dressing room. He didn't have to say a word. The rumpled state of his clothing told his mother everything.

"I demand that you repair the damage you've done to my daughter's good name." Mama was almost screeching.

"Damage that wouldn't have been done if you'd kept your voice down," Lady Thornton said.

Mrs. Rowland waved her finger in their hostess's face. "I am not content to sweep this matter under the rug and act as though your son hasn't defiled my daughter!"

If there was one thing Celia's mother was good at, it was putting on a show. Even though most of her audience had been forcibly removed, it was clear she wasn't about to quit the stage.

"Nothing happened, Mama. His Lordship didn't know I was here. He'd just discovered my presence and was about to leave."

She caught the look that Lady Thornton cast toward her son and braved a quick glance at the viscount before looking away again. All she could think about was the muscles she'd seen in that all-too-short glance. But it had been enough to make it clear that this man did not need to pad his clothing. Nor did he need to wear constrictive garments to hold in his waistline as her father had done when he was alive.

"I regret that you had to find out about my betrothal to Miss Rowland in this manner. We'd planned to keep it a secret for a little while longer."

She could only stare at Thornton in disbelief. She almost thought she'd misheard him until her mother let out a disgruntled snort.

"You will make an announcement tomorrow. We can't have people gossiping about my daughter."

Thornton nodded once.

"This isn't necessary—" Celia began.

Mama cut off her protest. "I'd expected better behavior from you." Her frown was almost laughable. Celia had no doubt that her mother was delighted, and everyone in the room knew it.

"Mama—"

"You'll be married soon. Before Christmas."

If the viscount was angry, he hid it well. "Before the beginning of the new year."

Her mother was going to argue, but Lady

Thornton spoke first. "Of course. We'll need time to prepare and to send out the announcements. And a special license will need to be procured."

That seemed to mollify her mother. Having trapped one of the wealthiest men in England into marrying her daughter, she'd want everyone to know about it.

Thornton turned his back on their mothers and gave her a bow. When he spoke, his voice was low, for her ears only. "We'll find a way out of this. You won't be forced into a marriage you don't want."

She searched his blue eyes for a hint of anger. He must think she'd planned this, and that thought caused her a pang of dismay. "Nor you."

With a nod, he turned to leave the room. He extended his arm to his mother, who took it with aplomb.

Her mother waited just long enough for the door to close behind the pair before allowing a grin to spread across her face. She rushed to Celia and took hold of her hands.

"That was well done! I never expected this from you. Placing yourself in the viscount's bed was a stroke of genius."

She tried to hold on to her composure as her mother clapped her hands together in glee.

"I must admit I was surprised when Lady Thornton came to collect you this evening. But now I see she had the same intention as I did."

Shock went through her. "You don't think… Did the two of you plan this together?"

Her mother waved a hand in dismissal. "No, of course not. But I did follow to see where you were going. When I realized she was bringing you here, I decided to wait to see what would happen. I was just about to retire when the viscount arrived."

She couldn't have heard correctly. "You knew this was going to happen? You saw the viscount enter the room and didn't stop him?"

Her mother's eyes narrowed. "Of course not. Who am I to thwart fate?"

"Fate? Mama, we can't trap the viscount into marrying me."

"It doesn't matter now. A fair number of people saw you in the viscount's bedroom. And when they discover he has arrived…" She raised one shoulder in a casual shrug.

"He can leave again before anyone learns of his arrival. No one needs to know why you were so upset tonight."

She started for the door, intending to go after

the viscount and Lady Thornton, but was pulled up short by her mother.

"You will do no such thing. For the first time in your life, you have finally done something right when it comes to your search for a husband, and I will not allow you to ruin it."

"We can't do this. It isn't right."

Her mother's gaze hardened on hers. "You've been reading too many stories about romantic love. It's about time you learn that such notions are fit only for fairy tales. Yours will be a marriage to be envied."

Her mother made her way to the door. Celia's hopes of leaving to find Thornton were dashed with her parting words. "I have no qualms about explaining why I was so upset. There will be no hiding what happened here tonight. Congratulate yourself, my dear. You are about to become the new Viscountess Thornton."

With that, her mother strode from the room, a satisfied smile on her face.

Celia collapsed onto the bed and stared up at the ceiling as her thoughts whirled. She knew her mother well enough to guarantee she would not willingly veer from this course. She only hoped the viscount would be able to devise a way out of this mess.

CHAPTER 3

ONE OF THE SERVANTS would escort Thornton to a bedroom that wasn't occupied, but first he needed to speak to his mother in private. He struggled to rein in his temper as he escorted her to her bedroom, refusing to give their guests another reason to gawk.

He vowed that he wouldn't yell as she opened her bedroom door and moved to the side to allow him to enter. He barely took in the surroundings of the pale yellow and lavender room, which hadn't changed since he was a young boy. He'd always enjoyed coming to visit his mother here, but now he could feel the control he held over his anger starting to come undone.

Celia Rowland wouldn't have been in his

bedroom if his mother hadn't arranged for her to sleep there. If she were any other woman who'd wanted to take advantage of the situation to trap him into marriage, she wouldn't have been so surprised by his presence. There was none of the archness he knew women displayed when they were playing a role, and he could tell her concern was genuine despite the moment of awareness that had passed between them when she'd stared at his body. If she'd meant to trap him, she would have gone out of her way to ensure she was well and truly compromised, but instead she'd wanted him to leave as soon as possible.

He ignored the little niggle of disappointment that he hadn't even gotten to kiss her before all hell had broken loose.

Somehow, he managed to keep his voice even when he faced his mother. "Were you really that desperate to have me wed that you would stage what just happened?"

She drew an audible breath and glared at him. He'd expected all manner of excuses from her, but not anger.

"Me? Why didn't you heed Saunders's warning? I don't know what type of adventures you get up to when you're in town, nor do I want to know, but

Celia is a gently bred young woman. To think that my own son would try to take advantage of her."

His indignation evaporated in the face of her own. "I didn't know she'd be there."

His mother's anger didn't abate with his protest of innocence. "Saunders has never been derelict in his duties and you'll never convince me otherwise."

He crossed to the small sitting area set up on one side of the large chamber and dropped onto the chaise longue.

"I was tired. He informed me you wanted to see me right away, but I told him I already knew what you wanted to speak to me about. He protested, but I insisted. He must have assumed you told me about Celia in the letter you'd sent." A part of him still couldn't believe that his mother was entirely innocent when it came to the fiasco that had taken place that night. "Why would you put her in my room? Surely you haven't invited so many people that we've run out of bedrooms?"

His mother sat next to him on the opulent lavender seat, her shoulders drooping. "I put her next to her mother. But I came upon Mrs. Rowland speaking to Lord Gravenhurst and could scarce believe what I was hearing. He was going to compromise her so she would be forced to marry him." She met Thornton's gaze. "I couldn't allow that to happen. Mrs. Rowland hasn't made her frustration a secret. She's arranged for all manner of suitors, but her daughter didn't accept any of them. Still, I couldn't allow Celia's hand to be forced in that manner.

The irony of the situation wasn't lost on him. "And instead, I compromised her."

"I didn't want this to happen. But you should know that Celia is a good match for you."

"It appears that everyone will get what they want except for Celia and me."

"And the odious Lord Gravenhurst. Oh, why did I invite him?"

He placed a hand over his mother's and squeezed it lightly. "Because he was a friend of the family."

She shook her head. "Not really. Your father didn't like him, but for some reason he felt it important to cultivate the man's friendship. He has power in parliament."

"Power that is waning."

His mother met his gaze and frowned. "Truly? So I kept up the acquaintance for no reason?"

He gave his mother's hand one last squeeze before releasing it. "How could you know?"

No, his mother wouldn't have heard the whispers that were spoken about the man. He'd buried two wives, and now his eyes were set on Celia Rowland. No matter what came out of tonight's events, he couldn't be sorry that she'd escaped the man's clutches.

He rose and stared down at his mother where she remained seated. She seemed so small, and her distress was genuine.

"Everything will be fine. I'll speak to Miss Rowland tomorrow, and we'll decide how to proceed."

"Do you think she'll end the betrothal before it's even been announced? I fear what her mother would do in that situation."

He bent and dropped a kiss on his mother's forehead. "Try to get some sleep. We'll sort things out tomorrow."

He wasn't surprised to find Saunders waiting for him outside his mother's bedroom. To his credit, the butler didn't betray a hint of censure and led him, in silence, to another bedroom.

Despite his parting words to his mother, Thornton didn't think he'd be able to sleep a wink that night. All signs of the fatigue that had led him to behave so carelessly had fled.

It was impossible to ignore the whispers the next morning when he made his way to the breakfast room. He'd finally managed to find solace from his spinning thoughts in sleep, but he was awake far too early for his liking.

His gaze swept over the many guests, far more than usual. Did his mother invite everyone in the county? It would figure that she would be hosting her largest Christmas gathering the year he committed such a faux pas as unintentionally compromising a young woman.

He called out greetings to everyone as he crossed the room to the sideboard. He didn't see Celia, but he did spy Baron Gravenhurst.

After piling up his plate, he made his way to the empty seat next to the man. His mother's revelation that Celia's mother had entered into an agreement with the baron to have him compromise—if not outright defile—her daughter angered him. He hoped his mother had been mistaken in what she'd overheard.

It didn't take him long to discover that wasn't the case.

Gravenhurst glared at him, not bothering to

hide his displeasure as Thornton took his seat. "I didn't know I would have a rival for Miss Rowland's affections."

Thornton met and held the man's gaze. "Miss Rowland and I have known each other for some time. She was a good friend to one of my sisters."

He let out an unseemly snort. "And was she also a special friend to you?"

"The last time I saw her, she was little more than a child. I don't make it a habit of robbing the cradle for female companionship." Unlike some people, he added mentally. Both the baron's wives had been young, just out in society. It rankled that this man, who was old enough to be Celia's father, had thought to coerce her into marrying him.

Gravenhurst merely shrugged and turned his attention back to his plate. "I can't say I blame you. I've never been good at waiting for the wedding night myself."

Thornton's fingers tightened on his fork. Regretting his decision to sit next to this man, he forced a mouthful of eggs down his dry throat. Maybe if he ignored the baron, he would stop talking.

But it was almost impossible to ignore the fact Celia had experienced a near miss last night. If not for his mother's quick thinking in seeing her out of harm's way, she could very well have found herself betrothed to this loathsome man this morning. He didn't want to contemplate such a fate befalling sweet, luscious Celia.

Gravenhurst leaned closer to him. "Of course, if you change your mind, I will have no problem taking her off your hands. I don't even care about her ruined reputation," he said with a wink.

Thornton's fork clattered onto his plate, but the baron was oblivious to his growing anger.

"Young man like yourself, you don't want to tie yourself down too quickly. Say the word, and she can be Lady Gravenhurst."

Over his dead body. Thornton met the baron's gaze, allowing ice to touch his words. "I don't know what you think happened last night, but you should stop talking right now. The next time you address me, I would advise you to remember that Miss Rowland is under my protection. I would have no qualms about calling you out."

He almost wanted Gravenhurst to defy his warning. Then he could plow his fist through the man's face.

CHAPTER 4

ELIA NEVER WANTED to leave this room again, but she knew her mother would never allow her the luxury of privacy. When a maid arrived with one of her outfits, Celia sighed and began preparations for the day.

It didn't matter that no one had seen the viscount last night. Many had seen her in his bedroom, and when they realized he was in residence… She shuddered at the thought that everyone would be talking about them. Gossiping and jumping to all manner of incorrect assumptions.

Assumptions that her mother would do everything in her power to encourage.

When the maid finished putting up Celia's hair,

she stood and braced herself for the day. But how did one prepare themselves to be at the center of a scandal? She knew many young women who would thrive under the speculation she was about to face —she'd met many of them during her last season. But she'd always had to be dragged out of her preferred hiding spot sitting on the outskirts of the many ballrooms she'd frequented.

For a fleeting moment, she thought she might be able to dart downstairs quickly, grab something to eat, and then retreat somewhere quiet where she could hide for the rest of the day. But when the maid opened the door to leave, her mother brushed past the young woman.

"Oh good. I thought for sure you were going to try to hide today."

And there went all thought of trying to find a reprieve. Celia knew this house much better than her mother, after all, since she'd stayed here several times when she was younger. She had no doubt she'd be able to find somewhere to conceal herself from everyone who would be speculating about what had happened last night.

She sighed as her mother tucked Celia's arm into her own and all but dragged her from the viscount's bedroom. To everyone who saw them, it would look like a show of support. But her mother grasped her arm a little too tightly, and Celia knew there would be no escaping her.

Walking into the breakfast room was worse than she'd imagined. The soft hum of conversation came to an abrupt halt, and every eye in the room turned to look at her. There must be at least twenty people present. If her mother didn't have such a tight grip on her arm, she would have turned around and walked back out.

Lady Thornton came to her rescue, crossing to her side and almost prying her from her mother's grasp. Together they walked over to the sideboard, the sound of whispers resuming as they passed. Mama followed closely, as though afraid Celia would somehow escape.

"I hope you had a restful sleep after last night's interruption. I should have told your mother that I'd temporarily moved you because your room wasn't ready. I never thought she would become so worried when she couldn't find you."

Celia didn't miss her mother's indrawn breath behind her, and she braced herself for a scene.

"I'm just glad Saunders was able to warn my son about the temporary change of rooms when he arrived early this morning."

Celia loved this woman. The whispers increased behind them, the dowager viscountess's words passing from person to person. With any luck, this would be the end of any discussion about forcing her and Thornton into a marriage.

"And where is Lord Thornton this morning?" Her mother's voice, much louder than necessary, set Celia's nerves on edge. She wasn't going to let this go. "Oh, there he is, sitting next to Lord Gravenhurst."

She caught the tense expression on Lady Thornton's face and the way the dowager viscountess's mouth tightened at her mother's mention of the baron. Celia couldn't help feeling as though she were missing something important and would have to ask Thornton about that later.

But at least the dowager viscountess had paved the way forward. If no one knew about the viscount accidentally getting into bed with her, they could still end the betrothal without any scandal. Perhaps at the end of the house party, when everyone left to return to their own homes in time for Christmas day, they could finally put an end to this nonsense.

Almost as though she'd summoned him, Thornton joined them. He invited them to join him at the end of the table, which was mostly unoccupied.

Lady Thornton led most of the conversation, trying to steer it away from Celia and Thornton. Celia noticed the displeasure on her mother's face and knew the morning's reprieve wouldn't last long. She'd demand a formal announcement be made in front of their guests or expose what had really happened last night.

Celia chanced a glance at Thornton, taking in his expression as he spoke to her three cousins who had moved down the table to join them. Lily, Iris and Violet. They would accost her or their aunt the moment breakfast was over. She dreaded to think what Mama would tell them about last night's happenings.

As though sensing her gaze, Thornton turned to look at her. His smile betrayed no anger at the situation in which they found themselves. It wasn't difficult to smile back at him.

THORNTON SOUGHT THE REPRIEVE OF HIS STUDY after breakfast.

His mother's statements had quieted the speculation about what had happened last night, but they all knew Mrs. Rowland wouldn't be content to let the matter rest. He would have to make the announcement about their betrothal later that evening or risk her telling everyone she'd found them alone together in his bedroom.

To say he was annoyed with the woman would be a vast understatement, but at least she'd given up her scheme to create a match between her daughter and Gravenhurst. If his announcement kept that from happening, then he couldn't be sorry about putting off Saunders's attempts to warn him.

He didn't have any work to do, but that didn't stop his annoyance when a knock sounded at the door.

Instead of calling out for the intruder to enter, he rose from his desk and strode to the door. If this was Gravenhurst, back to make lewd comments about Celia, he'd have no qualms about doing whatever was necessary to shut the man's mouth.

His anger returning to the surface, he swung open the door. He deflated when he saw Saunders standing in the hallway.

The butler raised a brow at Thornton's abrupt behavior, but he didn't comment on it. "Your mother has asked to see you in her sitting room."

Thornton blew out a breath. "Of course."

He wondered what more she would have to say to him, but at this point he would not ignore another of her summonses.

The door to the sitting room was closed. Normally his mother kept it open, but like him, she probably wanted a moment of calm away from their guests.

He didn't knock, letting himself into the room and moving to close the door behind him before he realized that his mother wasn't there. Instead, Celia waited by the window, gazing out onto the grounds. She turned and met his gaze.

He didn't close the distance between them, but he did take care to lock the door. The last thing they needed was another interruption.

"Your mother thought we should talk."

"By all means." He indicated she should sit in one of the chairs and then took his own seat in the chair that was next to hers at an angle.

He couldn't help but wonder what his mother meant to accomplish by arranging this secret meeting.

Celia sighed. "I need to apologize."

He raised one brow. "I was under the assumption you were as much a victim of your mother's matchmaking attempts as I."

"I have no idea what happened last night. Your mother assured me that you weren't expected but that if you did arrive home early, the staff were supposed to show you to another room."

"That was the plan. But I arrived late and brushed aside Saunders's insistence that I needed to speak to my mother. You know how that turned out."

Celia let out a sigh. "You're not to blame. I still don't know why your mother even insisted that I sleep in your bedchamber last night, but she was quite adamant that my room wouldn't do."

He watched her carefully, searching for even a hint she was lying to him. She wouldn't be the first woman to try to trap him into marriage by having him compromise her, after all. But he could detect nothing but honesty in her clear blue eyes. Her hands were clenched together in her lap, her knuckles almost white.

"I've tried to talk some sense into Mama, but she won't listen to me. I'm afraid she won't be dissuaded from this course of action." She shook her head, a small vee forming between her brows. "This behavior is most unlike her. She can't honestly believe that you and I…" She looked away, unable to complete that sentence. She took a deep breath and continued. "You shouldn't have to suffer for her overreach."

Her statement unsettled him. "Overreach is a harsh term, and unjust. You're a gently bred young woman, and your family lineage is impeccable. Wasn't your grandfather an earl?"

"Yes, but that doesn't mean I want to trap you into a marriage you don't want. Mama has been trying to find me a husband for some time, but I never thought she'd force a match."

He couldn't detect any sign that Celia was putting on a show for him. Still, he continued. "She did find us together, and neither one of us was fully clothed."

She blushed and looked away from him. He remembered again how she'd looked him over and knew she was thinking about that moment as well.

Finally, she met his gaze again. "I'm going to break the betrothal."

He could only stare at her, convinced that she was speaking the truth. This foolish, selfless woman would allow her own reputation to fall into ruins to ensure his happiness.

A stirring of emotion caught him off guard. It

was admiration. And along with that a pull that urged him to save her. But not because he was self-less. No, because it was her, Celia Rowland. And he didn't want to see her suffer.

"We shouldn't act too hastily. At the very least, we should wait until the rest of the guests depart in two days' time. We don't want your mother to share the real reason for our betrothal."

Celia shuddered. "Heaven forbid. Normally I'd say my mother would never do something like this, but she's being most insistent and I'm a little afraid that she might."

"So you'll wait?"

"Yes, but only until the other guests depart. I don't want this situation to get any worse than it already is."

He frowned, knowing that if his mother was to be believed, Mrs. Rowland had planned for a much worse scenario. And his mother had no reason to lie.

Clearly, he hadn't been able to hide the anger that threatened to erupt every time he thought of Gravenhurst's intentions toward Celia.

She narrowed her eyes and tilted her head to one side as though trying to read his mind. "There's something you're not telling me."

There was no point in hiding the truth from her. If her mother was willing to concoct such a horrible plan with Gravenhurst, it was best Celia was on her guard. He tried not to think about the fact he wouldn't be there to protect her the next time her mother tried something similar.

"I'm telling you this because you need to know so that you can safeguard yourself in the future."

Her eyes widened, but she waited for him to continue.

"I spoke to my mother last night. I was convinced at the time that she had planned what happened together with your mother."

She gasped. "Surely she didn't—"

"No. As she reminded me, Saunders tried to prevent me from heading to my bedroom without speaking to her first. But I was tired and convinced that whatever she wanted to tell me could wait until morning."

"She was going to warn you that she'd placed me in your bedchamber."

"Yes. And she was angry when she thought I was, in fact, trying to compromise you."

"I can imagine," she said with a wince.

"Once my own anger abated, I realized she had

done everything in her power to ensure I didn't… stumble upon you."

Their eyes met and held for a long moment before she blushed again and looked away. Neither one needed to say that he'd done much worse than just stumble upon her.

"You should know that your mother had hoped to force a match between you and Gravenhurst. She had planned to catch the two of you together and then demand that you wed."

She gasped, her mouth hanging open. "She wouldn't. She wasn't happy when I discouraged my suitors last season, but she never pressed me about it. Why would she do something like that?"

The thought of Celia having suitors disturbed him, but he pushed away his discomfort. He'd felt the same when his sisters were being courted. It was natural that he would also be protective of one of their friends.

"Mother overheard them planning. To protect you, she arranged to have you switch rooms so he couldn't carry out the scheme."

"And instead, only succeeded in ensnaring you in the tangled mess."

"I was angry, yes, but not any longer."

She searched his gaze, her furrowed brow telling him she didn't believe him.

"Celia," he said, leaning forward. "I would do anything to ensure you're not tied to that man. You deserve better."

She let out a soft sigh. "That may be true, but this is my problem, not yours. At the end of this gathering, I will give you your freedom. And since I am now of age, I will let Mama know that much as she might desire it, she can't force me to wed. Any future attempts on her part to force a match between me and another man of her choosing will only lead to my ruin. I will *not* be forced to wed."

He couldn't help but wonder why she seemed so vehement in her opposition to marriage. Was it that she wanted to choose her future husband herself, or was she opposed to the institution altogether?

Much as he wanted to, he wouldn't ask. "We have time. For now, our best course of action will be to announce our betrothal."

She winced but didn't disagree with him.

"We need to let your mother believe that her plan has worked so she won't tell anyone about our little misunderstanding last night. I am not just worried about myself. When we end this pretend engagement, I want your reputation to remain intact."

She smiled, but there was a sadness in her eyes that pulled at his heart.

"We'll find a way forward, Celia. One that will get you everything you want."

She looked away for a moment, swallowing visibly before replying. "Thank you for your concern."

She rose from her seat, and he followed suit. "You should leave first. When Saunders sees you, he'll fetch your mother. She'll escort me from her chambers so no one will know we were alone together."

He bowed and took his leave, but he didn't want to. He wanted to stay and try to reassure Celia that everything would work out well in the end. But how could he do that when, despite what he'd told Gravenhurst, it wasn't in his power to protect her?

You could marry her in earnest. You're attracted to her, and your friendship is a stronger foundation than many have when they wed.

He ignored the errant thought and strode from the room without glancing back.

CHAPTER 5

T HE DAY HAD BEEN AS DIFFICULT as Celia imagined. Despite the activities Lady Thornton had arranged to entertain her guests throughout the day, Celia's thoughts didn't stray far from what would happen over dinner.

Celia still couldn't believe her mother was behaving in such a manner. Yes, Mama had made no secret about wanting to see her wed, but to try to force her hand?

Dinner was lively, conversation flowing freely around them as they enjoyed the venison. Celia began to hope they'd avoided the whole ordeal. Perhaps the viscount's mother had convinced Mama not to pursue her current course of action.

Mama had been quiet over dinner, and Lady

Thornton had been masterful in encouraging everyone to share their plans for Christmas. That was only four days from now, but everyone would leave to make their way home in two days. Celia had to make it through that time without giving away the fact that her nerves were completely frayed.

She stole yet another glance at the head of the table, where Thornton was speaking to one of the guests seated to his left, an older widow whose name Celia couldn't remember. When his gaze sought out hers, there was a steely determination in his eyes that made her realize her hopes had been in vain.

The viscount rose, and conversation stopped as everyone gave him their attention. Celia glanced at her mother and couldn't miss the satisfied smile on her face.

She looked at Thornton again, marveling at how he could appear so calm. "I would like to take this opportunity to thank you all for joining us this year. What would Christmas be, after all, without one of my mother's house parties?" He paused, waiting for the murmurs of assent to die down. "I also have an announcement to make."

Celia straightened and tried not to cringe. Soon enough, everyone would be looking at her.

The viscount's gaze moved over everyone seated around the table. She'd thought there were a lot of people present at breakfast this morning, but the number seated along the long dining table made that group seem small.

She wondered if the dowager viscountess's Christmas gatherings were normally this large. She'd never attended before, even when Thornton's sisters were younger and she'd been a frequent visitor to the house.

Of course, it was just her bad luck that the first time she and Mama attended disaster had struck.

She kept her attention on Thornton, trying not to fret about all the witnesses to his announcement. It was impossible to ignore just how handsome he was. Of course, now that she knew what he looked like underneath his formfitting waistcoat and broad-shouldered topcoat, it was difficult to forget.

She'd fancied Thornton when she was younger, but she'd assumed that was just a youthful infatuation. During those summer visits, he'd been the attractive, dark-haired older brother to Emily and Julia. He'd always been patient with his sisters and, by extension, her. But his behavior now only cemented her good opinion of him. Any other man would have been angry about the situation in which they now found themselves. She'd expected bitter accusations about her scheming, perhaps even some pouting.

She should have known Thornton wouldn't behave in such a manner. He'd risen to the occasion with grace and aplomb. Their conversation earlier that day had confirmed that he wasn't happy about the current turn of events, but looking at him now, as he prepared to announce their betrothal, she could see no indication he'd been forced into this.

When his gaze reached her, a smile spread across his face. Her heart began to race when he lifted his glass of wine in her direction.

"I am very happy to announce that Miss Celia Rowland has consented to be my wife and will be the next Viscountess Thornton."

The silence that settled over the room was almost deafening, and she could feel the weight of all those gazes as everyone turned to look at her. Steeling her resolve, she raised her own glass in reply. With a tilt of her head and a forced smile, she took a sip of her wine.

Thornton's eyes remained locked on hers over his glass as he did the same. She was aware of movement around her as the rest of the guests raised their own glasses to toast to their happiness.

Thornton took his seat again, and the footmen sprang into action, removing their plates and then serving dessert. Plum pudding and an assortment of biscuits and macaroons were set out.

Slowly conversation resumed, but it was impossible for Celia to ignore the speculative glances cast her way. Mama, of course, was thrilled with the course of events, beaming with maternal pride.

Celia took a bite of the pudding but conceded she wouldn't be finishing dessert. She'd eaten little and imagined she would be starving come midnight, but it was impossible to ignore the nerves fluttering in her belly.

She wasn't accustomed to being at the center of so much attention, something which always left her uneasy. But beyond that, she'd come to an unsettling discovery. In that moment, when her eyes had met Thornton's as he'd made his toast, she'd become aware of an uncomfortable truth.

She'd thought herself past the youthful infatuation she'd once had for this man, but now she knew that wasn't true. Because a large part of her had wanted to believe his words were spoken in earnest. That he was announcing their marriage because he cared for her, perhaps even loved her. It was silly, the stuff of girlish dreams, but it was also her unfortunate reality.

The *tendre* she'd held for him had somehow blossomed into love. Perhaps she'd always loved him, but now she was aware of him in a way her younger self never could have imagined.

And because she cared too much to force him into a marriage he didn't want, she would have to let him go.

WHEN DINNER WAS OVER, THE WOMEN PROCEEDED to the drawing room, leaving the men behind. There would only be a short interlude before the evening's entertainment began, but it gave many the opportunity to swarm around her and demand answers to their questions.

Chief among them were her cousins, Lily, Iris, and Violet, who demanded to know every detail of her and Thornton's courtship. Celia tried to put them off, telling everyone she'd known the viscount since she was young and that everything had changed recently when they met again after not seeing one another for years. It wasn't a lie, but it lacked the details everyone wanted.

Finally, Lady Thornton rose and led the group to the music room. Bows of greenery were draped over the backs of the chairs that had been arranged around a pianoforte.

Celia made her way to the table that had been set up at the far side of the room with a large bowl of wassail. She took a deep breath, inhaling the rich scent of apple cider, spices, and brandy. She had a weakness for the warm drink and smiled widely at the footman who handed her a cup.

Her mother had secured seats for them at the front, but Celia chose to follow her cousins, who sat closer to the middle of the room. She could feel her mother's glare as she walked away.

The sound of animated conversation swept over her as many of the women indicated their intention to showcase their talents. Celia was relieved she would finally be able to settle back and enjoy the evening, secure in the knowledge that everyone's attention would no longer be fixed on her.

Lily sat to one side of her, Iris and Violet on the other, and they continued peppering her with questions. Asking her to share further details of her and Thornton's courtship, wanting to know how the viscount proposed and whether the wedding date had been set. They were less than content with Celia's vague answers.

Loud voices drifting through the doorway told her the men were finally joining them. She turned her back to the door, not wanting to be caught staring.

Lily squeezed her arm and leaned in to whisper in her ear. "I must admit I'm a little jealous. The viscount is the most handsome man here."

Celia agreed wholeheartedly. He was the most intriguing man of her acquaintance, and she'd come to know a fair number of them over the past few years as her mother did everything in her power to procure a match for her.

"He's also the youngest man here," she said.

Lily shook her head, her blond curls dancing about her face. "Don't be coy. You must give us more details. I will expire from curiosity."

Celia raised her brows. "Perhaps later, when there aren't quite so many ears around us."

Iris and Violet almost bounced in their seats. "Don't even think about excluding us. We don't care that Lily is the oldest."

When the men entered and settled toward the back of the room, it took every ounce of willpower

Celia possessed not to turn around and look for Thornton. Under other circumstances, she wouldn't have hesitated to wave a greeting to him, but now that there was so much talk surrounding the two of them, she didn't dare.

The dowager viscountess settled behind the pianoforte, starting the evening off with a beautiful rendition of "The First Noel." Celia had always enjoyed Lady Thornton's singing, having heard it many times in the past. The dowager's voice was deeper than that of many women's, lending a rich quality to the song that matched her playing. Celia's own voice was a moderately high soprano, which was ordinary in her opinion.

Her applause was heartfelt when Lady Thornton came to the end of the song. Thornton's mother rose and swept into a deep curtsy. This was a woman who was confident in her abilities and who didn't mind the attention that came with performing. Unlike Celia, who enjoyed singing and playing only in private or before a small group of acquaintances.

Lady Thornton gazed out over the group. "I'd like to invite anyone who wishes to have a turn. Who will be first?"

To Celia's horror, her mother rose. Mama didn't sing, which could only mean…

"I think my daughter should go first, all things considered."

And just like that, the relative peace of the past few minutes evaporated as everyone turned to look at her. Celia's thoughts raced as she searched for a reason not to perform for so many people.

Mama didn't give her a chance to come up with an excuse. "As you can all see, my daughter is shy and will need some encouragement."

She was going to kill her mother. Why was she doing this to her?

The polite applause and cajoling that followed her mother's statement gave her no choice. Despite wanting nothing more than to flee from the room, Celia took a deep breath and stood. The encouragements stopped then, and it was impossible to ignore the whispers. Some were from disgruntled women who'd wanted to showcase their own talents, and one person wondered if Celia could even play.

She'd be able to play, but she couldn't guarantee her voice wouldn't falter.

It was clear that she wouldn't be able to avoid the coming humiliation, so she might as well get it over with as quickly as possible. She gathered her hands together at her waist to keep them from shaking and made her way to the front of the room.

If she didn't make eye contact with anyone while she played, perhaps she could pretend this was one of those times when she'd played for Thornton's family. He'd even been there on occasion.

She lowered herself onto the bench, smoothing out her skirts. Her hands weren't shaking, something for which she was grateful. She ignored the sheet music Lady Thornton had piled for the guests. There was one Christmas carol she knew by heart, and she didn't want to prolong this ordeal by shifting through the music to find a different song. Unfortunately, it was also a relatively long song.

With a deep breath, she placed her hands on the keys, trying to convince herself this would be like all those other times she had played in this very room. But it was impossible to ignore the whispers. She was going to embarrass herself.

Movement to her left had her turning to see who was approaching. She expected to see her mother, or perhaps Lady Thornton was planning to join her. She never expected to see the viscount. While he'd watched her and his sisters perform on several occasions many years ago, he'd never once joined them. Could he even sing? If not, they would both be making a spectacle of themselves.

But she couldn't ignore the warmth that kindled inside her at his willingness to come to her aid. Again.

He smiled at her, causing her heart to flutter, but this time it wasn't caused by nerves. He turned his back to their audience and spoke in a low voice, for her ears only. "You don't need to be nervous. I've heard you perform, and you are more than up to the task."

She wasn't sure that was true, but with him at her side, standing next to her, most of the people would be looking at him and not her.

She took another deep breath and started playing the opening strains of "The Twelve Days of Christmas." The first few keys were rough, but it didn't take her long to fall back into the rhythm of the song. She'd played this many times and didn't really have to think about what she was doing.

Singing was another matter entirely. When she opened her mouth to begin, nothing came out. Fortunately, Thornton didn't wait for her lead and his rich baritone filled the room. She joined him on the second line of the song and their voices weaved together through the lyrics, melding perfectly. No one would guess that they'd never sung together before that night.

Her attention drifted from the keyboard. At first she looked down, not to help her play but to allow herself to concentrate on the song and not on the people who were watching them. But before long, her gaze drifted to Thornton as she watched him sing as though he made a regular habit of performing for others.

She didn't even realize that the rest of the guests had joined in, singing along with them, until she reached the very end of the song and her fingers stilled on the keys.

She smiled at Thornton, wondering why she'd never heard him sing before tonight. She remembered his sisters trying to get him to join them, but he'd never agreed.

She'd completely forgotten the audience until they broke out in enthusiastic applause. She tore her gaze from Thornton's, feeling the heat in her cheeks as she rose. She dipped into a curtsy and then took his arm as he escorted her back to her seat.

When she passed her mother, the secretive smile on Mama's face told her that she'd noticed Celia's reaction to the man. Everyone else would see that moment as proof that she and Thornton cared for one another, but Mama knew the match wasn't genuine. And apparently she now knew that Celia still cared for him, as she had when she was younger.

Celia settled back into her seat, relieved that she hadn't embarrassed herself. A steady stream of women took their turn singing and playing for the others. She couldn't let her guard down completely as she feared her mother would volunteer her for another song, but Mama must have realized she'd barely escaped public humiliation. If it hadn't been for Thornton's assistance, that outcome would have been certain.

Finally, Lady Thornton stood and thanked everyone for their participation. Celia couldn't help but notice the significant look she cast at her son before announcing the next portion of the evening's entertainment.

CHAPTER 6

OF COURSE, THERE WAS DANCING. His mother's Christmas parties grew more elaborate every year, and this was one tradition she'd instituted two years ago.

He stood to one side, chatting with some of the men, many of whom wanted to know if there was a gaming room. He promised to check with his mother and, if she hadn't planned one, to rectify the oversight himself.

While the guests milled about, most of the chairs were swiftly removed from the room. A few were placed in small groupings along two of the walls for those who wanted to sit, and when that task was completed, one of the older footmen took his place at the pianoforte. He had performed this task every year since his mother discovered the man had a natural talent for playing. He would play soft music while the guests conversed with one another.

He approached his mother and pulled her aside. "You've set up the card room?"

His mother sighed. "Of course. This isn't the first party I've hosted." She placed a hand on his arm. "But you'll remain?"

Against his will, Thornton's gaze drifted to Gravenhurst, who was staring at Celia with a slight frown on his face. He didn't particularly want to dance, but he would stay to keep the baron in line.

He nodded before rejoining the other group. His mother always set up the tables in the billiard room, and he told them they could proceed there.

He was surprised that only a few men departed, the rest opting to stay with their wives. He could only attribute their behavior to the sentimentality surrounding the Christmas season.

The footman had started to play a light tune that served as background music for the clustered guests. He knew that, as in previous years, most of the dancing would be done by the married couples and the young women who threw themselves into dancing with one another. They'd never behave in such a manner in London, of course, but here in the country, emboldened by the spirits Cook had added to the wassail, they'd have no qualms about enjoying themselves.

He gazed across the room to where Celia was standing with her three cousins, imagining they'd all join in the festivities soon.

He frowned when he saw Gravenhurst approach the group and bow. The man wouldn't dare ask Celia to dance with him…

Celia's gaze swept across the room before finally settling on him for a moment. And in her eyes he could see a plea for assistance. Given that she now knew this man's intentions toward her were far from honorable, she wouldn't feel comfortable dancing with him.

But when she looked at the baron again, the corners of her mouth lifted in a stiff smile. Dammit. Of course, she was going to accept. She was too polite to refuse him outright.

He didn't even realize he'd started to move, but when Gravenhurst raised a hand for Celia to take, Thornton was already at their side.

"Miss Rowland," he said with a bow. "I hope you haven't forgotten that you've promised me this first dance?"

Celia's expression warmed, her smile no longer

forced. "I thought perhaps you'd want to join the men who departed for other entertainments."

"And miss the opportunity to dance with you? Never."

He didn't even glance at Gravenhurst as he led her to the middle of the room, where two lines of women were already forming. He would be the only man in the set, but he had two younger sisters, so it wouldn't be the first time he'd have to entertain a group of females on his own.

The music became livelier, and soon he and Celia were moving through the figures of the dance, coming together and then parting again. There was no opportunity to talk privately, so they kept their banter light, conscious of the fact that the other dancers would be able to catch snippets of their conversation.

He could barely take his eyes off Celia throughout, mesmerized by her laughter and the joy radiating from her. He wasn't aware he was focused so intently on her until one of her cousins—Iris?—sighed loudly and commented to her sister that the two of them made a good match.

He should have been annoyed at the observation, but for some reason he wasn't. And he realized it was because his feelings for this woman were becoming complicated.

He started that dance thinking only to protect her from Gravenhurst, but by the time they reached the end, he realized that he wanted to spend more time with her.

They moved off to the side when the set was over, but he didn't leave. One glance at Gravenhurst told him the man was waiting for Thornton to do so, and he wasn't about to leave Celia unprotected.

He expected her cousins to surround them but saw that they were taking up their positions for the next set. His mother was deep in conversation with hers, so they wouldn't be joining them. Not that he expected Mrs. Rowland to protect her from Gravenhurst. She'd failed in that task once already, so he wasn't about to give her another opportunity to do so again.

They found two chairs that were unoccupied and settled into them.

"I didn't know you could sing." Celia gave her head a small shake. "I was fully prepared to make a fool of myself, and then I feared we'd both suffer that fate together."

"You wound me with your lack of faith."

Thornton was aiming for mock outrage, but Celia only laughed at him.

"You can hardly blame me for thinking that. All those times your sisters and I gave our little performances you never once joined us. Why was that?"

"My mother."

She tilted her head to one side. "I seem to recall her trying to cajole you into joining us on more than one occasion. I believed that you refrained because you didn't want to embarrass yourself."

He could understand why she'd thought as much. "It's quite the opposite, I'm afraid. Mother used to show me off all the time when I was a child, insisting we sing together whenever possible. Especially during her Christmas parties, which she's been hosting for as long as I can remember. I grew to hate it. Then when my voice deepened…" He shrugged. "I told her I'd lost the talent."

Celia smiled in sympathy. "I wish my own mother could be so easily put off. Honestly, I don't know what she was thinking. She knows I hate performing in front of large groups of people."

"She wanted to show you off."

Her mouth twisted in displeasure. "I'm sure it was more that she wanted to gloat about our betrothal. As though everyone here wasn't already talking about it." She shook her head. "At any rate, thank you for coming to my rescue."

"It was no great sacrifice," he said, realizing that he meant the words.

"Indeed, I never would have imagined our voices would meld together so perfectly."

That wasn't all Thornton wanted to meld together.

He cleared his throat and looked away, trying to tame his wayward thoughts. His attraction to Celia was almost embarrassing, but she was no longer the young girl he used to know. She'd grown into a very beautiful woman. One who'd apparently had many suitors.

"Do your sisters know?"

His thoughts scrambled for a moment, but she couldn't be asking him whether they knew about his growing feelings for her. "Excuse me?"

"Do your sisters know you have the voice of an angel?"

He scowled at the thought. "They never would have let me get away with not joining in on their little performances if they did."

Celia smiled. "I don't suppose they would have. Well, the secret is out now. They'll insist on singing with you the next time they're here."

"I'm sure I can mangle a song well enough to put them off that idea forever."

Celia laughed. "Were you always this amusing?"

He placed one hand over his heart. "Of course. Are you saying you didn't think I was amusing all those years ago?"

"Always." The warmth in her eyes as she looked up at him had him wondering what else she used to think about him.

"I think my sisters had a little contest between them about who could annoy me more. In fact, I wouldn't be surprised to learn that they still do."

Celia gave a little snort. Her hand flew to her mouth, and he found himself charmed.

"I'm glad you weren't annoyed with me. Honestly, I had the most horrible *tendre* for you." With a slight gasp, she covered her mouth again. "I did not just admit that to you."

He raised a brow, surprised. "How many glasses of wassail have you had tonight?"

She blew out a breath of laughter. "Just the one. I can't even blame my wayward mouth on an excess of spirits."

His gaze settled on her mouth for a moment. He hadn't realized just how plump her lower lip was. He wondered how it would taste if he took it between his teeth.

He shut down those thoughts immediately, but he couldn't stop himself from asking the next question. "So you no longer feel the same way about me. Have I aged so dreadfully over the years?"

She shook her head and swatted at his arm.

"Of course not. But I gave up youthful fantasies some time ago."

"And yet here we are, betrothed."

His reminder had the opposite effect of what he'd hoped to achieve. Celia closed her eyes as though he'd caused her pain.

"I'm so sorry you're being forced to go through this."

"Well, I'm not." He stood and held out a hand to help her from her seat. Then he tucked her hand into his elbow. "I'm sure no one would begrudge you a second glass of wassail. We must enjoy it while we still can."

She beamed up at him. "Yes, please."

Mama burst into Celia's bedroom the next morning just as the maid was about to leave.

Her mother's gaze swept over her outfit, a simple yellow day dress with small white flowers. "That will do," she said with a nod before turning to the maid. "My daughter will be going out this morning. Please see that her cloak and gloves are ready. She'll need to stay warm."

The maid curtsied and left the room to do as she'd been bid.

Celia frowned. She hadn't known Lady Thornton had planned any outdoor activities for the day. The estate didn't have a lake, so they wouldn't be going skating.

"Where are we going?"

Mama took hold of her hands, urging her to stand. "Not we. You and Lord Thornton."

Celia frowned. "I'm sure you're mistaken."

Mama let out a long-suffering sigh. "His lordship is going to be visiting his tenants today, something about handing out geese for their Christmas dinners. Apparently he's done it every year since he became aware some have been going without on Christmas."

Celia wasn't surprised to hear that. Thornton had always been generous with his family, so it stood to reason he would extend that kindness to his tenants. Still, her mother's revelation raised the man even further in her estimation.

"Who else will be going?"

"No one else. As his betrothed, he thought it prudent to introduce you to the families that live on his estate."

Given that their betrothal would soon be ending, Celia doubted that was true. "What did you do, Mama?"

"Fine," her mother said, throwing her hands up in the air. "I might have suggested it would be the perfect opportunity. And since some of the other guests were present at the time, he couldn't very well say no."

Celia cringed as she imagined his reaction to her mother's manipulations. "Mama, you should have left it alone."

"Nonsense. Now come, there isn't much time for you to have a quick breakfast before you're to meet him in the front hall."

Celia followed her mother from the room. As they made their way to the breakfast room, she tried to come up with a suitable excuse not to accompany Thornton.

By the time they reached their destination, she'd concluded there was no escaping the task. It would seem selfish in the extreme not to go with her would-be husband as he performed this very worthy errand. Still, she hated that they'd be forced to lie to even more people.

Her cousins were already seated and had saved a space for her. She went to the sideboard and made a quick plate of eggs and toast before joining them.

It was obvious to Celia that they wanted to press her for details about her relationship with Thornton, but her cousins couldn't ignore the people who surrounded them, leaning in a little too close to eavesdrop on their conversation.

Instead they made small talk, mainly sharing their favorite moments from the night before. Chief among them was the moment Thornton had surprised everyone by joining her for "The Twelve Days of Christmas." Conscious of the others listening in, she didn't mind sharing how nervous she'd been before he'd gallantly come to her rescue.

When she finished her eggs, she bid her cousins goodbye and made her way to the front hall. Thornton was already waiting for her.

She didn't miss the way his gaze swept over her and couldn't hold back the blush that crept into her cheeks. "I'm sorry to have kept you waiting," she said when she reached his side.

"I've only just arrived myself, so no need to worry."

The butler had her cloak draped on his arm, and she was surprised when Thornton took it from the man and helped her into it himself before donning his own. Amelia took her gloves from the butler with a smile, then fell into step with Thornton as they left the house.

The sun was out that morning, but a brisk wind had her shivering.

Thornton frowned. "Are you warm enough?"

She nodded. "The wind took me by surprise, but I like the winter air. It's invigorating."

They walked in silence the short distance to where the carriage waited for them. He helped her into the vehicle before climbing in after her. There were packages everywhere, but a small space had been kept clear on each of the bench cushions that faced one another.

Celia settled into her seat and waited for Thornton to do the same before asking, "How many families will we be visiting?"

He smiled at her. She had the impression that he was amused, but she couldn't say why.

"All of them. This is one of my favorite Christmas errands, but I'm sorry you were pressed into joining me."

"It's no trouble at all," she said, doing her best to ignore the way his good humor made him even more attractive. His blue eyes were bright with excitement. "But I do hate that we'll be lying to even more people."

"We won't need to lie. There'll be no reason to announce our betrothal to the tenants."

She realized he was correct. Even if they wondered about her presence, they wouldn't presume to ask. Content with that thought, she settled back into the cushions as the carriage made its way to the first house. To keep from staring at Thornton, she turned to look out the window. He did the same, but she couldn't help but feel the weight of his gaze several times throughout the drive.

HE'D RUN THROUGH THE GAMUT OF EMOTIONS THAT day. First, anticipation for his yearly ritual of visiting his tenants to ensure they would all have a happy Christmas. Then annoyance at Mrs. Rowland's further scheming to ensure he would have to take Celia with him.

When she joined him, however, he found that he enjoyed her company as they shared stories about past Christmases. They fell into an easy rhythm, with him presenting each of his tenants with a large goose for their holiday meal. Celia had insisted on carrying the second box to be delivered, a task the coachman had performed in previous years. It would contain various sweets for the families to enjoy together.

He'd been correct in telling Celia no one would

ask them outright why she was there, but her presence caused more than a few raised eyebrows and knowing glances.

He couldn't deny he was drawn to the way she seamlessly slid into the role his future viscountess would one day perform. And when she'd picked up one toddler who was pulling at her skirts, giving him her attention, the thought occurred to him that she would be a wonderful mother. He was wondering how many children they would have together when his reverie was disturbed by a clap on the shoulder from his tenant. The man nodded toward Celia then said in a low voice, "You've managed to find a good one there."

He let the comment slide, neither confirming nor denying the man's assumption. But the fact of the matter was he'd been thinking the exact same thing.

Celia turned to him and beamed, allowing the toddler to play with one of her curls. When he pulled a little too hard, she wrapped her fingers around his and brought his hand up to her mouth, placing a kiss on his palm. The child's mother swooped in then, apologizing as she took the little boy from her.

Celia laughed. "He wasn't the first, nor will he

be the last child to pull my hair. Please don't concern yourself."

They said their goodbyes then, and he led her from the house.

The emotion that dominated in that moment was confusion because he suddenly realized he enjoyed this task even more with her by his side. He enjoyed *her*. It wasn't just that he was attracted to her, and how could he not be with her blue eyes and blond hair and her luscious figure. He even liked the way the small mole at the corner of her eye highlighted how her eyes crinkled when she smiled. He also liked *her* as a person.

As the morning drew to a close, he found himself staring at her more and more. He didn't realize he was doing it until she reached up and patted her hair when they were seated in the carriage again. "Has a pin fallen out? Heavens, I must look a frightful mess."

"Not at all," he said, embarrassed at being caught acting like an infatuated youth. "I was just thinking that you looked a little cold." It was true that her cheeks and nose were tinged with red and her hair a little windblown, but that had only served to highlight her beauty.

She let out a sigh when the carriage pulled away

from the last house to return to the estate. "I suppose it is time to return to all the speculation and scrutiny."

Because she sat opposite him in the carriage, he could watch her without worrying about being caught. His mouth turned up in amusement. "There was plenty of speculation during our visits today."

"Yes, I know, but no gossip. And for the most part, everyone seemed happy to see me. They weren't looking for scandal."

He hated the flicker of pain that crossed her face. "I didn't realize the whispers bothered you so much."

Her mouth dropped open for a moment. "How could they not? Don't they bother you?"

"My dear, I'm unwed and in possession of a title. The whispers have surrounded me my entire life. They became particularly bad when I turned thirty." He lifted one shoulder in a casual shrug. "You grow accustomed to it."

Her fair curls bounced as she shook her head. "I can't see how. At any rate, the speculation will soon be gone. When the guests leave tomorrow, I'll tell Mama we've decided to end the betrothal."

Her words left a sour taste in his mouth. "Will we?"

"Fine, me." She looked away. "I'll break the engagement. Your reputation will remain intact."

"What of your reputation, Celia?"

She met his gaze. "Mama will be angry, but I'm now of age. Papa set aside some money for me. Of course, he thought it would act as my dowry, but it wasn't specifically set aside for that."

He could only stare at her as he tried to decipher her seemingly casual expression. Was this something she truly wanted, or did she think it was what he wanted? He was beginning to realize it wasn't, but he had to figure out her true feelings.

When he didn't reply, she looked away again. "If things are unbearable at home, I can find a small cottage somewhere where no one knows who I am."

He frowned, hating the idea of her walking away from him and everyone she knew. Sweet young Celia had grown into a temptress, and she wouldn't be safe out in the world alone. Away from him.

"Do we need to end the betrothal right away?"

She stared at him, her lips pressed together, before finally shaking her head. "There will be no point in continuing the pretense once everyone has left."

"What if I told you I think we're being too hasty? That I might want to continue with our betrothal."

Her eyes widened for a moment before narrowing again as she tried to decipher the true meaning behind his words.

"You needn't go to the trouble to protect my reputation."

She was so intent on righting the wrong that her mother had done to the two of them that she couldn't see what was truly happening.

"I'd like to perform a little experiment," he said.

"What type of experiment?" Her lips were still pressed tightly together. He'd have to see whether he could change that.

He indicated the spot next to her on the carriage seat, which was now cleared of packages. She nodded, and he moved into place beside her. They weren't far from the manor house, so they wouldn't have much time before the carriage reached its destination.

He left a respectable distance between them but positioned himself at an angle so he could still watch her as they spoke. He was happy when she mirrored him.

He extended one hand and waited. Celia bit her lower lip, an action that had him wanting to groan, before placing her gloved hand in his. Slowly, giving her time to draw back, he lifted their joined hands and placed a kiss on the patch of bare skin at her wrist. He lingered for a moment, his eyes fixed on hers.

A jolt of anticipation shot through him at the contact, but he held himself back. This was about discovering Celia's true feelings, after all. That anticipation tightened low in his belly when he saw the way her eyes widened at the contact, her breath quickening.

"Am I making you uncomfortable?"

She was silent for a moment, and he feared the worst. He was about to release her hand when she shook her head. "No."

"So you don't mind it when I hold your hand like this? When I kiss your wrist?"

He repeated the movement, and this time her slightly dazed expression was his reward.

"No."

His grip tightened on her hand. "I'd like to kiss you, Celia. May I?"

Her nod was immediate.

He leaned closer, stopping when their faces were only inches apart. "Are you certain you don't mind?"

"Thornton…"

The pleading note in her voice told him clearly that she wanted this as much as he did. He closed the distance between them, pleased when she met him halfway.

He meant to keep the kiss light, not wanting to scare her away. But then she made a soft sound of pleasure, and all his good intentions flew out the window.

The only parts of them that touched were their hands and lips, but he did deepen the kiss. When his tongue touched her bottom lip, she sighed and opened her mouth to accept him.

His skin was on fire, his need for this woman growing with every second that passed as their mouths moved together as if they had done this a thousand times before. She leaned in closer, and her other hand went to his shoulder, but still he resisted the overwhelming need to pull her close.

The sudden jolt of the carriage coming to a halt brought an end to their kiss. He pulled back, as did she. Their gazes locked for several long moments.

He still held one of her hands, and her other hand rested on his shoulder.

"Celia—"

The rattle of the carriage door handle had him releasing her and moving away to preserve Celia's modesty.

Her eyes examined his, and he feared he was about to grab hold of her again, modesty be damned. To prevent that from happening, he stepped down from the carriage first, then turned to help her down.

His fingers tightened on hers to get her attention, but she refused to meet his gaze again. Red tinged her cheeks, but this time he didn't think it was caused by the cool air.

He placed her hand in the crook of his elbow and led her back to the house. When they were a few steps away from the footman who had opened the carriage door, he leaned in close and whispered, "I'd say that experiment was a success."

She didn't reply but the shiver that went through her was all the confirmation he needed that she agreed.

CHAPTER 8

IT WAS TWO DAYS BEFORE CHRISTMAS, which meant his mother's guests would be leaving today. Everyone except Celia and her mother, who had been invited to spend Christmas with them. Celia's cousins would be leaving with one of the other guests, an older couple who had volunteered to see them safely home.

Celia had avoided him for the rest of the day after he'd kissed her, but she wouldn't be able to do so once everyone left.

It seemed that the entire household had woken early and were in the breakfast room that morning. Along with enjoying the grand array of food the servants had set out, many were milling about the room, taking advantage of the last opportunity for conversation before they departed.

His mother sat at one end of the long table and he at the other. And while he had the opportunity to speak to most of the people present, he was acutely aware that Celia was still avoiding him.

She'd arrived late that morning and had given him a quick smile before joining her cousins. He'd caught the way the eldest of the three—Lily?—glanced his way several times during the conversation, which meant she wanted to talk about their relationship. But her frustrated sighs told him Celia was changing the subject.

He didn't regret kissing her yesterday. Her surprise had been genuine, but she'd warmed quickly and had enjoyed it as much as he did.

No, he didn't regret it because it told him exactly what he needed to know. Celia Rowland was drawn to him. She liked him, and he knew that she found him attractive—he was haunted every night by thoughts of how she'd looked at him when he'd left the bed they shared briefly and imaginings of what could have happened if they hadn't been interrupted. He only hoped he'd been successful in convincing her to wait before ending their betrothal.

Gravenhurst was the first to bid his goodbyes to the room at large. Thornton followed him from the room, waiting until they were nearly at the end of the hall before calling out to the man.

Gravenhurst turned and glared at him. "Come to gloat some more?"

The annoyance in the man's voice sparked Thornton's anger. He'd hoped this would be a civil discussion, but it was clear that wasn't to be.

Thornton narrowed his eyes and fixed them on this man who had thought to steal Celia away. "If I hear even one rumor about Miss Rowland, I'll know it came from you."

Gravenhurst scoffed. "What would you be able to do about it?"

Thornton moved closer. "Make no mistake, you will regret it. You might have had friends once, but your biggest allies have turned their backs on you. I can make you a pariah."

Gravenhurst clenched his jaw. Thornton could tell the man wanted to argue but couldn't. His time doing whatever he wanted was in the past. No one would take Gravenhurst's side in a battle between the two of them.

The man gave a stiff nod and turned away. Thornton watched him leave. It took almost a full minute for his anger to cool enough for him to even think about returning to the other guests.

Before he reached the breakfast room, Celia's cousins emerged, followed by the couple who was going to be taking them home. The three curtsied and then hurried past him, giggles trailing in their wake. Thornton bowed to the older couple and turned to watch them go, wondering what it was about him that had amused Celia's cousins.

When he entered the room, most of the guests had stood and were in the process of taking their leave of one another. He moved to stand next to his mother, who stood to one side of the entrance. Together, they thanked the guests for coming and wished them safe travels and a happy Christmas with their families.

Thornton kept glancing at Celia, who now sat beside her mother. He willed her to look up at him, but she kept her gaze averted. That bothered him more than he'd admit because he couldn't tell what she was thinking.

He needed to convince her not to end their betrothal, although he couldn't say why he wanted it so much. She'd grown into a beautiful young woman and had been of age to marry for some time now. The difference in their ages was no longer insurmountable, and he couldn't look at her without wanting to take her into his arms.

She was still sweet, of course, but she also had a determination about her that he admired. And her honor was without question.

Their betrothal had stemmed from an unfortunate turn of events, but he could no longer look at it that way. Because he realized that the misunderstanding that had led to the two of them sharing a bed, albeit briefly, could very well be the best thing that had ever happened to him. That would ever happen to him.

Good grief, he was in love with Celia Rowland.

When the final guest left the room, he strode to Celia's side. When she looked up at him, it seemed as if she was surprised to see him there. He searched her gaze but couldn't tell what she was thinking.

"We'll talk when the guests have all departed," he said.

Celia replied with a nod before looking away again. That simple action told him she still planned to end their betrothal. He wanted to pull her away now, but he had to make an appearance in the foyer to see the guests off.

As if on cue, a footman appeared to his right. "Lady Thornton is waiting for you, my lord."

He gave the man a nod and turned to leave. He didn't miss the satisfaction on Mrs. Rowland's face as he walked past her. It was clear she had no idea what her daughter intended to do. He only hoped he could convince her otherwise.

CELIA WATCHED THORNTON GO WITH A HEAVY heart. There was no sign of the easygoing man she'd seen the day before when they were visiting his tenants. Instead, he'd been so serious.

He confused her. She'd been under the assumption he wanted their forced betrothal to end. Then he'd kissed her, and she'd allowed herself to believe there might just be something more between them. But he hadn't said as much, and just now he hadn't shown any indication that he wanted to court her in earnest.

She took a deep breath to steady her nerves for what was to come. She couldn't allow sentimentality to sway her, and she wouldn't force the man's hand.

After she broke their engagement, she and Mama would leave. She couldn't say when she'd see him again. Now that his sisters were wed and living in the north of England, she would have no excuse to visit again. And she most definitely wouldn't be attending another of his mother's Christmas house parties.

Mama approached to her left and twined her arm through Celia's.

Celia allowed her to lead them from the room so the footmen could clear the remains of the morning meal. But when her mother started to turn toward the foyer, clearly intent on joining Thornton and his mother in bidding the others adieu, Celia tugged on her arm to lead her in the other direction.

Mama tilted her head in question.

"You and I should speak in private before the others return."

Mama considered for a few seconds before nodding her head. "Of course, my dear."

Letting out a breath of relief, Celia led her to the library where they'd be far enough away from the front hall and all the hustle of the departing guests. No one would overhear their conversation.

She had to choose her words carefully. Her mother couldn't guess that she intended to end her pretend engagement to the viscount before the last guest had departed—when it would be too late for her mother to let slip the secret that she and Thornton had been caught together in his bedchamber. Some of the guests were wondering if that had happened, but they didn't know for certain. Celia intended to keep it that way.

But she did need to clear the air with her mother. Her heart was already breaking at the thought of having to end the betrothal. Her mother's scheming to try to force her into a match was a betrayal she had never expected.

She closed the door behind them and turned to face her mother.

"What is the matter, dear?" Her mother's brow was furled in what appeared to be genuine concern. But after learning what Mama had planned with Lord Gravenhurst, Celia wasn't sure she knew this woman at all.

"Lord Thornton told me what happened."

She expected to see guilt, not confusion on her mother's face. "Don't we already know what happened?"

"You can stop pretending, Mama. He told me you'd planned to have Lord Gravenhurst compromise me to force me into marrying him."

Celia saw it then, the flicker of guilt. Then her

mother gave up all pretense and settled into one of the armchairs that were placed before a roaring fire.

"What do you think you know?"

Celia slumped into the chair opposite her mother. A part of her had held on to the hope this had all been a misunderstanding, but now it appeared as though everything was true.

"Were you truly that desperate to have me wed that you—" She had to take a deep breath before she could continue. "You arranged with Lord Gravenhurst to have him compromise me."

Her mother shook her head. "No, it wasn't like that—"

"Lady Thornton overheard you. That was the reason she spirited me away from my room and had me sleep instead in Thornton's room."

"She told you that?"

Celia wanted to laugh at her mother's outrage, but her disappointment was too great. Her mother's betrayal too much. "Of course not. I imagine she wanted to shelter me from the truth that you would go to such lengths to force me into a union I didn't want. She told her son what happened, and he, in turn, told me. To warn me that I needed to be careful in the future."

Her mother leaned forward. "I didn't intend to

allow that to happen. I did have that conversation with him—"

Celia opened her mouth to interrupt, but her mother cut her off.

"No, let me finish. Please."

Celia said nothing and so her mother continued.

"I knew about your feelings for the viscount."

Heat flooded Celia's cheeks. "My youthful infatuation with him, you mean. I outgrew those fantasies years ago."

Her mother's smile was sad. "No, you didn't. You wanted to believe you had, but I could see the truth in your face whenever I brought him up. When I mentioned the invitation to this party, you were excited to attend."

"The party, Mother, not because of the viscount. And what does that have to do with you arranging to have Lord Gravenhurst compromise me?"

Mama winced. "I never should have had that conversation with him. But you should know that I never intended to allow him to go through with it."

Celia rose to her feet and walked away as her disappointment turned to anger. She had to take several deep breaths before turning around to face her mother again.

"I'm going to need you to tell me exactly what you thought would happen. I'd considered myself fortunate to have a parent who didn't feel the need to force me into accepting a marriage proposal I didn't want. But this…" She shook her head. "I am sorely disappointed to discover I was wrong."

Clearly alarmed, Mama leaped to her feet and closed the distance between them. When she reached for her hands, Celia drew back.

Her mother wrapped her arms around her waist. "I made sure to have that conversation with the baron in Lady Thornton's hearing. Then I stood guard down the hall from your room to ensure it didn't happen. I was convinced she was going to confront me about it. I wanted to convince her to work with me to try to make a match between you and her son."

Celia shook her head in disbelief. This sounded more like something her mother would do, but to bring a third party into it? "What were you thinking, Mama? This could have gone horribly wrong. What if Lord Gravenhurst had succeeded?"

"No… no. That never would have happened. If he didn't listen to me and go away, I would have raised the roof before he even got near your room. He would have been forced to leave in disgrace."

"But instead Lady Thornton spirited me away."

"Yes."

"And when Thornton arrived home, you had no difficulty allowing him to enter the same room in which I was sleeping."

Her mother's shoulders slumped. "I was only thinking about how much you cared for him. And I know he was a good brother to Emily and Julia. I thought he would make the perfect husband and that everyone would be happy."

"You played with all our lives, and now Thornton and I have to pay for it."

"But—"

"No, Mama. No matter what happens now, you must promise me you won't interfere."

She could see the moment her mother realized what Celia planned to do. And she could also see her struggle with the desire to ensure the marriage went forward.

"I will never forgive you if you say anything about what happened."

Mama's mouth trembled, then she took a deep breath and nodded.

"You won't interfere anymore? You won't tell

anyone that Thornton has compromised me, no matter what happens?"

"I thought my actions would end in you being happy. Clearly I was wrong. I won't do or say anything."

Celia nodded and walked past her mother. Mama reached for her, but Celia wasn't ready to forgive her. Because of her mother's actions, she'd come to realize that her infatuation with Thornton was, in fact, love. And she would have to set him free.

CHAPTER 9

THE LAST GUEST HAD FINALLY DEPARTED. Thornton stayed in the doorway just long enough to watch the carriage begin to make its way down the drive before leaving to find Celia. He needed to speak to her as soon as possible.

Sensing his mood, his mother didn't try to stop him.

When he looked in the breakfast room, a footman told him she had gone to the library with her mother.

When he entered the library and saw Mrs. Rowland sitting in an armchair, her head in her hands, he feared he was too late. He couldn't make himself ask what had upset her, so he stood there for several moments, fearing the worst.

His mother must have followed him because she entered the library as well. She took one look at Celia's mother and asked if something was the matter.

Mrs. Rowland shook her head, then grimaced. "Celia is angry with me. Given the way I've behaved, I can't say that I blame her."

He wanted nothing more than to chastise the woman himself, but it wasn't his place. And from the devastation on the woman's face, it was clear Celia had already said everything.

"I need to speak with her," Thornton said.

Mrs. Rowland shook her head. "She left me here some time ago. I imagine she's returned to her bedroom."

He began to turn, intent only on finding her, but his mother placed a hand on his arm to stop him. "I can ask one of the maids to go find her."

"There's no need. I'm here."

Thornton turned to see her standing in the doorway. She took a deep breath as she stepped into the room, and Thornton braced himself for what was coming. He tried to meet her gaze, to let her know that they needed to speak before she went forward with this course of action, but she kept her gaze fixed firmly on the floor.

"Celia—"

She shook her head and locked her eyes on her mother, who had risen to stand at her entrance. "His lordship and I have spoken, and we've reached an agreement. We've decided that our betrothal—"

"Should be extended for a period of time."

Celia turned to stare at him, her eyes wide. "But—"

He kept his eyes locked on hers. "If we rush and marry before the start of the new year, tongues will wag in earnest. I would save your daughter from even a hint of gossip."

Celia shook her head, the blond curls that framed her face bouncing with the forceful movement. "That's not what we settled on."

"We should leave them to talk," his mother said. He didn't even turn in her direction as she and Celia's mother left. He could hear their footsteps and murmuring voices disappearing down the hall.

Celia stared at him for several seconds before speaking. "I thought we decided it would be best if I ended the betrothal after everyone left."

"Did we?"

She let out a shaky breath. "Yes, we did. If you're worried about my reputation, no one need know that the engagement is over right away. But we need to set things right with both my mother and yours."

Doubt had him reconsidering their interactions. What if he'd been mistaken about Celia returning his feelings? He wasn't the first man to want to marry her. Perhaps he wouldn't be the last.

"Is the idea of being married to me so abhorrent to you?"

Her eyes widened. "No, of course not. It would be an honor to be your wife."

He took a step closer. "Just an honor? Nothing else?"

She looked away.

"Celia?"

She let out a sigh and met his gaze again. "I've come to… care for you. You're a good man, and you don't deserve to be forced into a marriage you don't want."

He could feel the doubts scattering with every word she spoke. "What about what you want? Do you want this marriage?"

She looked down at her hands, which she clutched at her waist. "It doesn't matter what I want. We're in this position because of my mother's scheming. You shouldn't have to suffer for it."

He could only shake his head in disbelief. "And what if I don't want you to end things?"

She sighed again. "I must be the one to end things so you can move forward without anyone questioning your honor."

He took another step closer. She still couldn't see what he was saying. "I think we should get married." He placed a hand over hers, causing her to stop fidgeting. "I *want* to marry you, Celia. Unless, of course, there is someone else…"

Her brows drew together, and she stared at him. He began to worry that sweet Celia's heart was already engaged elsewhere.

"No," she said when she finally spoke. "There is no one else."

"And you don't find the idea of marrying me objectionable?"

She shook her head, a look of wonder creeping onto her face. "Only a fool would object to marrying you."

"Well, then Celia Rowland, since you are no fool, I am asking you to please do me the honor of becoming my wife."

Her mouth gaped open, then snapped closed. "But my mother… you must hate her."

He shrugged. "I'm not overly fond of her, no.

And I question her lack of judgment in the way she was going about trying to find you a husband. But my feelings for her are irrelevant. It is you I wish to marry, not your mother."

She examined him, her gaze locked on his, and he knew she was looking for any sign he might be lying to her. She wouldn't find any.

"Are you sure?"

He smiled. "It appears we're going to get our fondest wishes for Christmas this year."

Her head tilted to one side. "I find it difficult to believe you wished for a wife."

He shrugged. "It was always going to happen, but not quite so soon. Then I happened upon a certain bundle in my bed and found myself wanting to see her there again and every night after that."

Celia laughed, and the sound sparked joy within him because it meant she was going to accept him.

"You could have any woman in England."

"That might be a slight exaggeration, but it doesn't matter. I want you. And if I must, I'll compromise you again."

When he opened his arms, she moved into them and raised her head for a kiss. "By all means, my lord."

He took her mouth on a laugh, but all amusement fled when she sighed and pressed her body against his.

Finally, he had Celia Rowland exactly where he wanted her. The last thing he wanted was to let her go, but the sound of voices increasing in volume told him their mothers were returning.

He let her go with great reluctance but tucked her hand into his arm. They were both smiling when their mothers returned.

"Perhaps a spring wedding?" He glanced down at Celia.

"Spring sounds wonderful," she said, beaming up at him.

CHAPTER 10

S PRING DID SOUND WONDERFUL, but it also sounded so far away. She and her mother would be spending Christmas with the Thorntons before returning to their homes. From that point forward, she would only see the viscount when he called on her.

After the bustle of the past few days, it was nice to spend a quiet day together. It was also frustrating because Mama and Lady Thornton seemed to go out of their way to ensure she and Thornton weren't alone together.

She was still angry at her mother, but she would forgive her in time. Everything had worked out beyond her wildest expectations, after all.

After dinner, they made their way to the

drawing room. Mama and Mrs. Rowland sat off to one side, snippets of their conversation catching Celia's ear. They were discussing the need to read the banns and when they should have the wedding.

Thornton, who sat next to her on the settee, could only shake his head. "They seem to be more excited than us."

She shook her head. "That isn't possible."

He smiled at her, and she had to fight the urge to swoon.

"I almost didn't come to Mother's house party this year and put it off as long as possible. I wasn't in the mood for all the singing and festivities. And after our first meeting—well, I wasn't in the best of moods that night."

She winced. "At least now we are free from the prying eyes of people who wanted to dissect our relationship."

"Indeed," Thornton said. "I must say that my sisters will be sad not to have been here."

"Was there a reason they didn't come? I was looking forward to seeing them."

"Apparently they were snowed in. I hope they're able to arrive for the new year. Mother will be sad if she doesn't see them at all for the season."

Celia looked over to where Lady Thornton was

laughing with her mother. "She doesn't look sad to me."

He laughed. "No, I don't suppose that she does. But that will change soon enough when you and your mother have gone home." He turned back to her, his gaze softening. "As will I. I'd originally planned to return to London after the new year, although I'm not sure why. Most of my friends have returned to their own homes, and the city holds little in the way of entertainments of late. Surrey seems to hold much more interest for me this year."

From the amusement that lit Thornton's eyes, it was possible she might have swooned just a little. Others had paid her similar compliments, but only this man could get such a reaction from her.

A hint of melancholy touched her heart at the reminder their time together, for the near future, would soon come to an end. "If you change your mind after I leave, you must tell me. We can still end the betrothal. And come spring and the beginning of the season, I'm sure there will be much more interesting gossip to entertain people."

He frowned, but his voice was light when he said, "Am I going to have to compromise you in actual fact to keep you from trying to escape?"

She must have drunk too much wassail that

evening. Why else would she have leaned closer to him and said, her voice matching his low pitch, "Perhaps you should."

When she realized what she had just proposed, heat crept into her face. But instead of being scandalized, Thornton's gaze locked on to hers and seemed to heat. "Perhaps I should."

She needed to get away from this man before she said or did something that would embarrass her further. It was taking every ounce of her willpower not to close the small gap between them and kiss him. If their mothers weren't in the room, she might have done just that.

A quick glance in their parents' direction assured her they hadn't overheard their conversation. With a soft sigh, she stood. Thornton followed suit, and all eyes turned to her.

"I think I'll be retiring for the night."

"Are you all right, my dear?" Lady Thornton asked.

She rushed to reassure her. "I believe the late nights from the past few days have finally caught up with me."

She turned to curtsy to Thornton. It was almost impossible to believe this man would soon be her husband.

He took hold of one hand and placed a kiss on her wrist, his warm lips resting momentarily on the exposed skin above her glove, his gaze locking on to hers. "Good night, Celia."

Flustered, she dipped into a curtsy and all but fled from the room, chastising herself all the way back to her bedroom. As her conversation played over in her mind, she couldn't hold back a groan of embarrassment.

She'd invited him to compromise her. What had happened to her common sense? Even worse, what if Thornton thought her a wanton?

She tossed and turned for some time, unable to dispel her worries, before finally falling asleep.

SHE HAD TO BE DREAMING. WHY ELSE WOULD Thornton be in her bedroom, sitting on the edge of her bed?

She rose to a sitting position and stared at him for several long seconds before finally finding her voice. "This is a dream."

Thornton leaned closer and placed a hand on her cheek. His thumb stroked along her lower lip. "Not a dream," he said softly.

The shiver that went through her body gave credence to his words.

She stared up at him. "You came. I never imagined you would."

"After that invitation, I'd be a fool to stay away. But I won't proceed unless you tell me you want this as much as I do. We can wait until we're wed to go any further."

She had no idea what instinct led her to take his thumb into her mouth, but the way his gaze darkened as she sucked on his thumb told her that he didn't mind. He slid his hand away after several seconds.

"I am a hairbreadth away from losing control. You must give me the words—I don't want to presume."

"Please stay." Two days ago she never would have imagined uttering those words, but in that time she'd come to realize just how much she cared for this man. She wanted to give him everything.

He drew in a shuddering breath. "You know what I am proposing?"

She nodded. "That we make love. And yes, I would very much like you to continue."

The press of his mouth on hers was her answer, and a thrill of expectation shot through her.

But then he kissed her the way he had in the carriage, sliding his tongue into her mouth to deepen the kiss. She'd always been slightly uncomfortable with the idea that men kissed in this way when Thornton's sisters had teased her about how delightful it was after they wed. She hadn't believed them, but she'd been very wrong to doubt them.

The way Thornton's tongue slid against hers was more sinful than she could have imagined, and she moaned in a way that should have shocked her.

He pulled back and gazed down at her, his eyes dark, reflecting the need she could feel growing within her.

"If you don't want me to——"

She dragged his mouth down to hers before he could continue, afraid he would disappear just as quickly as he'd appeared. "Don't you dare stop," she said against his lips before sliding her own tongue along his lower lip.

With a groan, he reciprocated, and they spent several long, delicious minutes kissing.

She let out a small shriek when he shifted her onto her back, but he swallowed the sound before pulling back to gaze down from where he hovered over her.

"This is your last chance to ask me to stop."

She shook her head. "Ravish me, my lord."

One corner of his mouth curved upward in a wicked smile. "You have no idea how much I've wanted this," he said, dropping a kiss on her cheek before moving to kiss the side of her throat.

Oh, she had an idea because she'd wanted it as much as he did. Wanted him. But she'd never even allowed herself to dream it was possible. Now she could recognize that the reason she'd never been able to settle on one of the many men her mother had paraded before her was because none of them could compare to the fantasy of this man.

But he wasn't a dream. This was very real.

She arched under his touch when he cupped one of her breasts.

"You've definitely grown up, Celia." He dropped kisses along the bodice of her nightgown and then gave the material a sharp tug. She'd hated how large her breasts had become. Hated how men seemed fixated on that part of her. But now, as they were bared to Thornton's hot gaze, she found herself disliking them a little less.

And when he took one of her nipples into his mouth, white-hot pleasure streaked through her. Words failed her as he took his time lavishing kisses over her breasts. She made a soft sound of disappointment when he rose to stand and struggled up onto her elbows.

"Don't leave."

"I have no intention of leaving. But first…" He strode over to the door and turned the lock.

Shock took over as she realized that anyone could have walked in on them. She tried not to picture her mother flinging open the door as Thornton was kissing her breasts, unable to hold back a twinge of embarrassment at her wanton behavior. Thank heavens at least one of them was still thinking.

He jammed the chair from her dressing table under the doorknob for good measure, and she stifled a giggle. Apparently the viscount was picturing the same scenario as her.

When he turned to face her, his brows were drawn into a frown. She realized she'd drawn the bed sheet up to cover herself and released her grip on the fabric, allowing it to slide down to her waist.

"Much better," he said.

The heat in his gaze did much to ease her embarrassment. What made it disappear altogether was watching him begin to disrobe.

With each garment, her anticipation grew. She'd already seen his bare chest that first evening.

This time, she didn't look away as he watched her reaction when he finally drew his shirt over his head.

More than anything, she couldn't wait to touch him. No, this wasn't a dream because her imagination wasn't this good.

Her breath hitched when his hands moved to the fall of his trousers. He stopped, one brow raised in question. He was asking her if he should stop. In answer, she took a deep breath, stood, and allowed her nightgown to fall in a puddle around her feet.

His movements quickened then, as though he couldn't wait to finally shed the last of his clothing.

When he stood completely naked before her, she couldn't stop the heat from rising to her cheeks. He was hard, his erection rising away from him. She'd heard about this too but found herself hesitating, unsure what to do now.

She wanted to touch him all over but didn't know if she should. She couldn't help but think that perhaps she should get back onto the bed and pretend she wasn't experiencing the sinful emotions that seemed to have taken hold of her.

She didn't realize she'd closed her eyes—she could still see him clearly in her mind's eye—until she felt his finger under her chin, tilting her face up to meet his.

She opened her eyes and his gazed bored into hers. "What are you thinking?"

She wanted to demur, to tell him it was nothing. But if she was going to marry this man, she didn't want to begin their relationship on a foundation of lies.

"I'm wrestling with what I want to do and what I think I should be doing."

"Meaning…?"

"I'm feeling decidedly unladylike. I want to touch you, but I'm not sure if I should."

By way of reply, he took hold of her hand and placed it squarely in the center of his chest. The heat rising from his skin almost scorched her hand.

"I plan to touch you *everywhere*, and I hope you'll reciprocate."

Almost of their own volition, her eyes dropped to his member before rising again to meet his.

He answered the question she couldn't ask. "Yes."

Never in a million years would she have thought herself brave enough for this. But she wasn't with just any man. She was with Thornton, and in his presence, she felt as though she could do no wrong.

Aside from that, he clearly wanted her to touch him, but he would never force her.

She started slowly, spreading her hands across the hard muscles of his chest, then across his abdomen. She hesitated, and he must have thought she would go no further for he took her mouth in another searing kiss and tugged her closer so their bodies aligned. She gasped at the feel of his skin burning into hers. Kissing this man was pleasurable when fully clothed, but when they were both bare, the pleasure was indescribable.

He cupped one of her breasts again, and in an act of bravery, she reached down to grasp his manhood. His hiss of breath had her releasing him again immediately.

"I apologize—"

By way of reply, he grasped her hand again and brought it back down to encircle him.

"I was surprised, Celia, not in pain. It is more painful if you *don't* touch me."

CHAPTER 11

SHE WAS GOING TO BE THE DEATH OF HIM. He hadn't expected it, so when she wrapped her small hand around his length, the intense pleasure took him by surprise. But he most definitely did not want her to stop.

"Don't scream," he said before scooping her into his arms and carrying her to the bed. The feel of her smooth skin against his left him heady with need.

He placed her on the bed's surface with great care before lying down next to her. Then he proceeded to touch every inch of that skin he could reach, allowing his mouth to explore her glorious breasts. She reciprocated in kind, leaving behind her reservations.

When he couldn't wait any longer, he rose onto his arms over her. He should have prepared her with his hands or with his mouth but he feared he wouldn't have the restraint to do so without spilling all over the sheets. And he most definitely wanted to be inside her tonight.

He stared down at her, enjoying the way her breath came out in short pants as she toyed with the hair at the nape of his neck.

"This next part is going to hurt. I'm sorry."

She smiled up at him, no hint of trepidation in her eyes.

"I know. But I also have it on good authority that it will be even more pleasurable afterward."

He didn't want to know who'd shared such information with her. If it was one of his sisters... His mind shied away from completing that thought, and he refocused on Celia.

The first touch of his member against her wet folds had both of them releasing soft sounds of pleasure. Thankfully, she was wet. Her face scrunched in pain when he sank into her, and it took all his strength not to move.

She was tight, and he had to master himself so he wouldn't spill immediately. He had no idea what it was about this woman, but she affected him like no one else.

A full minute must have passed before she tilted her head to one side. "Is that all there is?"

His bark of laughter surprised them both. "No, my sweet Celia, there is more. I wanted to make sure you were no longer in pain."

She raised one of her legs, settling it over his, and he let out a groan as he sank deeper into her.

"I think I'm ready. It doesn't hurt anymore."

Thank heavens for that. He placed a hand below the knee of her leg and hitched it higher to encircle his hips. She followed suit with her other leg, cradling him within her body.

He couldn't resist kissing her again as he began to move. She was still at first, but within moments was moving with him. A soft mewl escaped her lips, and he leaned back to look at her, worried she was still in pain. But the expression on her face was that of a woman who very much enjoyed what they were doing.

Knowing how sensitive her breasts were, he began to knead one as he continued to thrust, doing everything in his power to move with care. She might not be in pain, but she would be sensitive.

"Isaac," she said on a low moan.

The sound of his name on her lips sent a jolt of pleasure straight to his heart. Very few people used his Christian name, not even his mother. But he found that he very much liked it.

He wouldn't be able to last much longer. Keeping his weight on one arm, he released her breast with reluctance and moved his hand between them. He circled that sensitive area above where they were joined, doing everything in his power to ensure she found her release before he did.

After only a few strokes he was rewarded by her swift intake of breath, and then her entire body clenched. The feel of her wrapping even tighter around his length caused him to lose what little control he had left, and he spilled inside her body.

They stayed like that for several long moments. When her eyes opened, her gaze was wide with wonder.

"I never expected…" She gave her head a shake, letting out a small laugh. "I suppose you'll have to marry me now."

He rolled to one side, taking her with him and tucking him into his side. "It would be my pleasure and greatest honor."

Thankfully, that would be soon. He'd been so

caught up in her pleasure and in his own that he hadn't pulled out of her as he'd planned.

Perhaps he'd be a father within the year. The thought should have filled him with horror, but instead a smile spread over his face as he pictured Celia round with his child. But he couldn't risk that happening before they were wed.

"We'll arrange to have the banns read right away and be married in a month."

She lifted her head, her radiant smile doing much to ease the guilt he felt at not being able to wait. "Spring was too far away," she said. "I was never going to last that long without you."

He twined his hand in her hair and returned her smile. "I couldn't agree more."

HE STAYED IN CELIA'S BED MUCH LONGER THAN HE'D intended, and only managed to make it back to his room just before the sun began to rise.

No sooner had he crept into his own bed than his valet entered. The man's eyes swept over the bed, which wasn't nearly as rumpled as normal. He raised a brow but didn't say a word as he headed for the dressing room.

"We have guests, and your presence has been requested in the drawing room."

Thornton frowned, wondering which one of his mother's guests had returned. It had better not be Gravenhurst.

"Who is it?" He rose and joined his valet in the adjoining room, watching as the man picked out each item of clothing for the day.

"The footman didn't say. Apparently it's supposed to be a surprise."

Thornton grinned. That must mean that at least one of his sisters had made it down, which would please their mother to no end. That's all she wanted for Christmas, after all—to see her family all together for at least a few days.

When he was finished dressing, he thanked his valet and headed for the drawing room. The sound of voices echoing down the hallway told him that his guess had been correct. Even better, when he entered the room he saw that both Emily and Julia were there, as were their husbands.

"Isaac!" Both his sisters leaped from their seats and barreled into him, embracing him from each side.

Emily gave him a mock frown when she pulled back. "We'd hoped to surprise you, but it seems you've taken the wind out of our sails. I can't believe you and Celia are to be married!"

He looked over to where Celia was sitting on the settee, a serene smile on her face.

"Within the month. We've decided to have the banns read and then have the ceremony the following week."

Julia looked over at her husband. "We hadn't planned to stay that long, but perhaps we can change our plans."

Mother was beaming from her seat next to Celia on the settee. "We do still have some of your gowns here for your visits. I'm sure we can manage."

Emily placed one hand over her belly. "I imagine they'll still fit, but perhaps they'll need to be let out by the end of the month."

"Congratulations, Emily," Thornton said, dropping a kiss on his sister's cheek before turning to congratulate his brother-in-law.

Mother and Celia rushed to Emily's side while he greeted the two men.

"I think you've managed to overshadow our announcement," Thornton said, clapping Emily's husband on the shoulder.

"Nonsense. I'm surprised you didn't hear the

shrieks when your sisters learned about your betrothal. It was almost deafening."

Thornton turned to watch the women, who were huddled together, chattering away.

He didn't realize he was staring until Julia sidled up next to him and elbowed him. "I recognize that look. You're in love."

Celia joined them and smiled at him.

Emily sighed loudly. "We're so happy for the two of you. Celia has fancied you for as long as I can remember."

Color rose in her face, and Thornton smiled fondly at her.

"Well, back then she was far too young for me to think of in that way. But trust me, I took notice of her right away upon our meeting again."

"You must share all the details," Emily said. His sisters each took one of his arms. "But first, break-fast. I'm starving."

Celia lifted one shoulder in a small shrug, and he couldn't help but wonder if she would, indeed, tell his sisters everything. He tried not to think about what else she would share with them as he led his sisters and the small group to the breakfast room.

CHAPTER 12

Christmas morning

ELIA WOKE WITH A SMILE ON HER FACE.
Everyone had stayed up into the early hours of the morning to welcome in Christmas. The pianoforte had been brought into the drawing room, and they'd sung carols for a good portion of the evening, played whist, and chatted. Finally, Emily had announced she was exhausted. Declaring that she didn't want to see anyone until midmorning at the earliest, she'd retired with her husband. After her departure, everyone had wandered off to their own bedrooms.

Celia hadn't expected Thornton to join her—he

wouldn't risk it a second time. Still, unable to fall asleep, she'd waited up for some time.

It was silly, but she missed him. Now that they had a future together, she couldn't wait for it to start.

She called for a maid, who helped her to dress and pin up her hair. She was on her way downstairs to join the others for breakfast when it occurred to her that this would be her future home.

She stood in the doorway for several moments, taking in the scene before her. Thornton and his family were seated around the breakfast table, talking and laughing. He was teasing Emily by proposing the most ridiculous of names for her baby, and with each suggestion, both she and Julia laughed even louder. Her two friends had always meant the world to her, and joy unfurled in her chest at the knowledge they would soon be her sisters.

Lady Thornton saw her first and called out a welcome.

Every eye in the room turned to her, everyone calling out their own greetings. She'd been the subject of similar scrutiny when Lady Thornton's guests were still in residence, but she felt no unease with these people who were soon to be her family.

Her gaze settled on Thornton, and she didn't care that her smile could only be called sappy.

She caught the way Emily and Julia were grinning at her as well as the dowager viscountess. When Thornton rose and approached her, she realized they were waiting to see her reaction.

Thornton stopped before her, and she gazed up at him, curious. "What is happening?"

He pointed up, and it was then she saw the mistletoe hanging in the doorway. Thornton plucked a white berry from the small branch before leaning down to place a quick peck to the side of her lips. When he pulled back, his gaze was intense. "Walk with me for a moment."

Making a point not to look at anyone else in the room, she nodded and took his arm. He led them to the drawing room.

He moved to stand in front of her, staring down at her. She couldn't help but take note of just how handsome he was, as she did every time she saw him. She didn't think it was possible for him to appear otherwise.

"That mistletoe wasn't there before," she said, thinking about the knowing looks from Thornton's sisters and feeling a twinge of embarrassment.

"No. Mother's never been one to put a woman in a position to attract attention she doesn't want."

She shivered, imagining Lord Gravenhurst taking advantage of such an opportunity. "But she's changed her mind now that the guests have gone?"

One corner of his mouth lifted in a knowing smirk. "I might have arranged that myself."

She could only shake her head in disbelief. "I should admonish you for embarrassing me like that, but in truth I didn't mind." She hesitated a moment before adding, "I missed you last night."

His blue eyes darkened. "And I you. But we've already taken one chance. I don't want you to fall with child before the wedding."

She sighed with disappointment but knew he was right.

He took one of her hands in his. "I didn't have anything to give you for Christmas."

He placed his other hand against her cheek, and she nuzzled into his palm.

"Nor I you. I expected to spend Christmas day at home."

He shook his head. "You've already given me so much. Given how our betrothal started, and your belief that I wished to be rid of you—"

"I—" She started to interrupt, but he moved his

hand and placed his fingers against her lips. He didn't drop them until she nodded to indicate she would allow him to finish.

He reached into his coat pocket to retrieve something. "I *didn't* have anything to give you when I arrived. I never imagined I'd find my future bundled underneath my bedsheets that first night. So I spoke to my mother, and together we decided there was only one thing to do."

She tilted her head in curiosity but had no idea to what he was referring.

He held out his hand. Nestled in his palm was a delicate gold ring with a rather large pearl mounted on it.

She gasped. It wasn't customary for a man to give his intended a betrothal ring, but she had to admit that his gesture touched the romantic inside her.

"This ring belonged to my grandmother. My father gave it to my mother when they became engaged, and now I'm passing it on to you with my mother's blessing."

She opened her mouth, then closed it again, too overcome with emotion to speak.

He smiled and raised her left hand. "We might need to have it resized." With care, he slid the ring onto her finger, and to both their surprise, it fit as though it were made for her.

She stared down at it for several moments, overcome with love for this man. When she met his gaze again, she could see a slight frown where before he'd been happy.

"Of course, I can buy something more ornate. I know it is a simple setting—"

This time, it was she who placed her fingers over his lips to stop him from continuing. "I will not have you saying anything negative about my ring. It is perfect… and so are you. I love you, Isaac."

His concern disappeared, replaced by a doting expression she didn't think she'd ever tire of seeing.

"I love you too, Celia. Happy Christmas."

He kissed her then, and she returned it without hesitation. She didn't care who walked in on them. She loved this man, and she wanted the whole of England to know.

EPILOGUE

November 1817

CELIA MADE HER WAY to the drawing room, pleased with the excuse to escape Lady Thornton's attentions, even if only for a little while. Her mother-in-law's annual Christmas party was only one month away, and she'd wanted Celia to feel as though her input was valued on every detail of the upcoming house party.

Every minute detail.

Honestly, it was an annual affair. How many decisions needed to be made? She'd wanted to tell the dowager viscountess to do what she'd done every year, but the look of excitement on the woman's face had stopped her.

But now her cousin Lily was here for a visit and Celia had leaped at the excuse to take a moment away from the small stack of menus the house-keeper had asked her to approve.

Celia smiled as she swept into the room. Lily seemed to be deep in thought and so she dropped onto the settee next to her cousin. "I'm so glad you're here. If I had to look at another menu, I was going to scream."

Lily let out a sigh and unease settled over Celia. "Has something happened?"

Lily bit her lip. "I needed to speak with you."

Celia grasped her cousin's hand. "Of course. You can tell me anything."

"It's about Lord Seaford. I think he's going to propose."

Celia frowned, wondering at Lily's obvious concern. "Would that be so bad? He's been courting you for several months now. I thought you liked him."

Lily leaned back against the settee and closed her eyes. "I thought so, as well."

"Then what is the issue?"

Lily met her gaze. "You are."

Celia shook her head, confused by her cousin's words. "Me? I've said nothing about Lord Seaford.

I barely know the man. He seemed nice enough when Isaac introduced us this past spring. Very respectable."

"That is the problem. I don't want someone respectable."

Her cousin wasn't making any sense. "You're going to have to explain this to me. Surely, you're not saying you want to wed someone disreputable?"

Lily blew out a long breath. "No, of course not. But I want a man who looks at me the way your husband looks at you. A man who loves me."

A twinge of dismay went through her at Lily's obvious distress. "That can come in time. It took Isaac and me a little while to realize our feelings for one another."

Lily laughed. "You've had a *tendre* for Thornton for as long as I can remember."

Heat rose in her cheeks. "I won't deny that's true. But I also know that you feel the same way about Lord Seaford. Or at least I thought you did."

"He's so polite, almost distant with me. So staid and careful. I want someone who will sweep me off my feet."

"Well, I can tell you that scandal is highly over-rated. I was very dismayed when Thornton was first forced into declaring we were going to be wed."

"But it worked out in the end."

"Yes, but what if it hadn't? I believe Lord Seaford is going about this the right way, giving the two of you the chance to know one another."

Lily leaned forward. "I can't deny that he's very handsome."

Celia lowered her voice. "Don't repeat this to my husband, but I think so as well. And…" She hesitated, unsure if she should continue.

"And what?"

"Isaac was dismayed when he heard that the Earl of Seaford was courting you. Apparently, he has a reputation for being a rake."

Lily sank back into the settee's cushions again. "That makes it even worse. Perhaps he's worked through whatever youthful wildness he possessed and now that he's ready to settle down, he's become boring. He has always been circumspect with me."

"Has he kissed you?"

Lily let out a snort. "He's kissed my hand. Does that count?"

Oh dear. Perhaps her husband had been mistaken about Seaford's reputation. "I can't tell you what to do. Have you shown him you want him to kiss you?"

Lily shook her head, her blonde curls bouncing

in joyous counterpoint to her somber mood. "How would I do that? I've smiled, laughed, leaned in a little close to him. Nothing."

Now it was Celia's turn to sigh. "How long has he been courting you?"

"Six months!"

Celia winced. "What is your heart telling you?"

The corners of Lily's mouth turned down. "I like him a great deal. And until I'd seen the way Thornton behaves around you, I thought we could make a good match. But I've discovered that I'm selfish. I want him to look at me the way your husband looks at you and I fear that will never happen."

Celia pulled her cousin into a quick hug. "The only advice I can give you is to listen to your heart."

"What if my heart and my head can't agree?"

Celia wished she could ease her cousin's dismay. "I'm afraid that only you can answer that question."

A HIGHWAYMAN FOR CHRISTMAS

Christmas Scandals

Book 2

ABOUT THIS BOOK

Lily Rowland has no choice but to reject the Earl of Seaford's marriage proposal. No one can deny the man is handsome, with his dark hair and dark eyes that flash with a hint of something that lies deeper beneath the surface. But despite the fact they have become good friends, the oh-so-proper earl can never give her what she wants…passion.

Simon took one look at Lily Rowland and knew she'd be his. But after months of resisting the temptation to throw her over his shoulder and carry her to a dark corner to do deliciously wicked things with her, he realizes he's made a tactical error. Because Lily doesn't want the respectable gentleman he's pretending to be. She wants the rake he's hiding from her.

Which leaves him with no choice this Christmas but to kidnap Lily to prove he can give her exactly what she craves.

❄

CHAPTER 1

December 1817

"I'm afraid I cannot accept your proposal."

With those words, an almost deafening silence settled over the room. Lily Rowland had to look away from the man who was seated at the other end of the settee, a respectable amount of space between them. A pang of remorse struck her, and she wanted to snatch back her refusal. Give him another answer.

She liked the Earl of Seaford a great deal. And heaven knew the man was handsome with his dark hair and dark eyes. At times she'd wanted to believe she could feel those fathomless eyes pierce through to her very soul. But those moments were fleeting, a product of her overactive imagination. Lord Seaford had always been circumspect in his behavior toward her, and he'd never once strayed beyond the bounds of social convention.

When he'd taken up residence on a neighboring estate six months ago, the entire area had exploded with speculation. No one knew why the handsome —and wealthy—young earl had chosen to move into one of his smaller holdings in Berkshire. His sister and mother stayed there during the winter months, but he'd never visited.

The resulting gossip when he began to court Lily had run through the neighborhood.

She'd had a disappointing first season that year. Seaford hadn't attended any of the usual events that spring. But they'd met at the very end of the season when Lily and her sisters visited Clara Howe, the earl's sister, before leaving London.

Lily had known his family for several years now since Clara was very close to Lily's youngest sister, Violet. That rainy afternoon in June was the first time she'd met Clara's brother.

When the earl joined his mother and sister in Berkshire, Lily's sisters had teased her relentlessly, saying that Seaford had followed her to the country. And when he'd called on her soon after, Lily realized her sisters were correct. She'd started spinning fantasies about how the handsome and enigmatic Earl of Seaford had taken one look at her on that rainy afternoon in London and decided he wanted her to be his countess.

But Lily's unease only increased with each passing month when it became clear that something vital was missing from the handsome earl's courtship.

He was attentive and everything a young woman could want in a suitor. Everyone would think her mad for turning down his marriage proposal. Without a doubt, her father and her sisters would question her sanity.

But when she thought about her future, Lily wanted what her cousin had found. Beyond the respect and regard of her husband—which Seaford could certainly give Lily—Celia Rowland had Viscount Thornton's love.

Celia had narrowly avoided being caught in a compromising position with Viscount Thornton last Christmas during the dowager viscountess's annual Christmas house party. They'd managed to distract everyone from the speculation about what might have happened when the viscount declared their intention to wed.

Celia had later confessed to Lily that he'd been forced into making that announcement, but it was clear to everyone who saw the two of them together that their relationship had grown beyond that scandal. They were in love. Seeing the way Lord Thornton looked at his wife… Lily wanted that for herself.

She'd hoped to find that with Lord Seaford, but it was clear there would never be heat in his eyes when he looked at her.

She glanced at him again and almost changed her mind when she saw the way his brow furrowed in confusion. Forcing back the urge to reach for his hand and tell him she'd made a horrible mistake, she looked away and took a deep breath.

She'd come to consider the Earl of Seaford a friend. Clara Howe's kind older brother. Friendship in marriage could only be a benefit, but she wanted so much more than that.

Of late, it had become increasingly obvious that something was amiss between them. Maybe turning down his proposal would fix the uncomfortable silences that had become more frequent whenever they were together.

"May I ask why?"

The words were spoken without a hint of emotion, which only served to confirm she'd made the right decision.

"I'd like to think we have become friends over the past few months."

He frowned. "Which means we will suit well in marriage."

She drew in a deep breath, trying to gather courage for what she needed to say. How truthful should she be? For a moment, his eyes dipped to her chest. But when he met her gaze again, there was no evidence of the heat she'd often seen on Lord Thornton's face when he looked at his wife.

She forced the words past her dry throat. "There is more than friendship between a man and a woman in marriage."

He looked away for several seconds. She waited, hoping he would say something—anything—to change her mind. To show her there was more than comfortable companionship between them.

"I can be patient. I'm sure we will... suit... in that area as well."

Disappointment threatened to crush her. She rose to her feet, and he did so as well. Of course he did. Seaford would never flout social conventions.

"We can discuss this again after we're married—"

"No," she said, cutting him off.

His mouth flattened into a line as he waited for her to continue. She wanted him to argue with her, convince her she was wrong about him. But his every action only served to underscore the truth. This man might come to love her, but she feared the emotion would be no different than what he felt for his sister.

"I want passion."

His posture stiffened, but she couldn't regret her outburst. Seaford couldn't give her what she needed, so it was best to let him know in no uncertain terms that her decision was final.

"What do you know of passion?"

His words were clipped, and finally there was a hint of heat in his eyes. If only that heat were directed at her. Instead, she couldn't help but think he was judging her. Perhaps he thought her wanton.

"Personally? Nothing. But that doesn't mean I don't want it. Crave it with every fiber of my being. I want what my cousin Celia has with her husband. I want people to take one look at me and my future husband and know that we are in love."

"I—" He opened his mouth to reply.

She spoke over him. "I know you don't think of me in that way, which is why I must turn down your offer of marriage."

Well, at least she'd finally forced him to drop his polite mask. But what replaced it was cold and more than a little frightening. If she didn't know better, she'd say he was angry with her.

She closed her eyes and took another steadying breath. He hated her now. Perhaps that was for the best. Seaford could never give her what she wanted, and it was time she gave up the fantasies she'd been spinning in her mind about this man.

She expected him to take his leave. Instead, a muscle jumped along his jaw, and he took several steps toward her. Shock held her frozen in place.

She stared up at him, and it was clear now that he was angry. No, furious. But this was Seaford, and he wouldn't hurt her. She stiffened her spine, waiting for him to tell her he'd misjudged her. That she wasn't the type of woman he wanted for a wife.

"I'm going to change your mind."

She stared at him in shock. There were emotions swirling in his eyes now, but she couldn't name them.

Before she could say anything else, he offered her a curt nod and left the room.

She stared after him, an uncomfortable realization settling over her. She had underestimated this man.

She couldn't help but remember her cousin's words when Lily had spoken to her recently. Celia had told her that her husband was concerned about Seaford courting Lily because the man had a reputation for being a rake. She'd dismissed Celia's warning because it didn't seem possible. The Seaford she knew could never be called a rake. But maybe she was wrong?

She dropped onto the settee, dread settling in the pit of her stomach. Her thoughts were mired in confusion. Was it possible she'd only seen one side of the man and that he possessed depths he'd been hiding from her?

No, she thought with a shake of her head. If he was hiding that side of himself, then she should be congratulating herself for having escaped unscathed. Surely only misery would come from being married to a man who thought nothing of throwing himself at all manner of women.

Then why did she want to chase after him?

She jumped when the front door closed with an unnaturally loud bang.

The silence that followed was broken by the

sound of quick footsteps before her sisters burst into the room.

Iris lowered herself onto the settee next to her. "What happened? Did he propose? Father said he was going to ask you today."

Violet sat on Lily's other side. "Did he change his mind? He'd still be here if he asked you… wouldn't he?"

Lily was unable to hold back her tears.

CHAPTER 2

*N*ever had Simon failed in such a spectacular fashion. He'd miscalculated—badly. But he wasn't going to quit the field.

He wanted Lily Rowland, and by God, he would have her.

If Miss Rowland thought him lacking in passion, she would soon learn the opposite was true. Gone was his farce of acting the part of a proper gentleman for her. Gone was his belief that he had to hide who he really was. To hide the fact that he wanted her with a desperation that wasn't gentlemanly. That wasn't nice.

No, from this point forward, he was going to take what he wanted. Lily couldn't know what she was asking for, but he was going to show her that he was more than capable of being passionate. He only hoped she was prepared to discover his true nature.

He stormed into the house, his temper still hot. But he wasn't angry with Lily. No, he was furious with himself. He'd been the worst sort of fool. Somehow he'd convinced himself that he needed to become someone he wasn't in order to gain the hand of the woman he wanted. Instead, he'd driven her away.

He swung the greatcoat from his shoulders and handed it, along with his hat and gloves, to the waiting footman.

"Please ask Hastings to see me in the study."

His words were clipped, and the young man turned immediately to find Simon's valet. At least he hadn't yelled.

He made his way to the study and poured a measure of brandy. It was only afternoon, but given the horrible mess he'd managed to make of his only attempt to woo a woman, no one would blame him for doing what he could to steady his emotions.

The past six months had been a special kind of hell for him. Being so close to the woman he wanted to make his own and forcing himself not to touch her.

At least he hadn't told anyone he planned to propose today. Hastings knew, of course, but his mother and sister expected him to propose at Christmas. That had been his original plan, but he'd become impatient. He wanted the matter of courting Lily behind him so he could have her as his wife. In his home and, more importantly, in his bed.

He'd given up all female companionship after meeting Lily earlier this year. He didn't regret that decision. He'd had his fill of women for years now, but Lily was the only gently bred young woman he'd met who stirred the beast within.

At first, he thought it was her beauty that captivated him, which had seemed odd. He'd met all manner of eligible young women who were as beautiful, perhaps even more so than her. But his instincts all sprang to attention when Clara introduced him to her good friend's oldest sister.

Those instincts had told him that the young woman standing before him, her blond hair curling about her face, her blue eyes gleaming with appreciation—nothing he hadn't seen before in countless other women—would belong to him. And not just for one night but forever.

He tossed back his drink and began to pace.

That was how his valet found him several minutes later.

Hastings rapped softly at the door and then let himself in without waiting for an invitation. He took one look at Simon and sighed.

"I take it this afternoon did not go as you'd hoped."

Simon laughed; he couldn't help it. The situation was absurd. "I am a case study in irony."

Hastings's brows rose. "That means…?"

"She refused me because she thinks we're *friends* and she wants *passion*." The words sounded bitter on his tongue. "Apparently she doesn't think she can get that with me."

He gave his valet credit for not laughing at him.

"You're not a man to give up so easily."

"Of course not. I'm going to give her exactly what she wants." One corner of his mouth lifted as he thought about all the ways he could show Lily that he was more than up to the challenge she'd laid before him. "She's thrown down the gauntlet, and I am honor bound to show her that I am more than capable of giving her exactly what she wants."

"Of course you are, my lord."

Simon ignored the hint of dryness in his valet's tone. The man had been with him for enough years to know that the one area in which the Earl of Seaford was *not* lacking was in passion.

His smile turned into a full grin as a plan began to form in his mind. "I'm going to need your help."

Hastings inclined his head. "Just say the word."

CHAPTER 3

*L*ily slipped into the morning room to find that her sisters were already hiding there. Father had been in a grumpy mood all day. It was now midafternoon, and soon they'd be leaving.

Normally the three of them spent their time in that room gossiping about what was happening in the neighborhood while working on their needle-work and drawing. But a dark cloud had settled over the house on what should have been a happy day.

Violet and Iris were standing side by side next to the window and turned at her entrance.

Iris let out a sigh. "It doesn't appear that it will snow."

"No." Violet's shoulders slumped. "We'll be

trapped in the carriage, listening to Father's complaints the whole way to Lord Seaford's estate."

Lily winced, guilt stabbing at her. "Father never liked house parties. I don't know why he agreed to attend this one."

Iris tilted her head to one side. "Do you not? We all thought you were going to marry the earl. So of course when his mother and sister invited us to spend a few days with them before Christmas, he jumped at the opportunity."

"He didn't precisely jump," Lily said, remembering the reluctance with which their father had agreed to go with them.

"Given his reaction last year when we suggested he join us for the Dowager Viscountess Thornton's annual Christmas gathering, it was as good as an exclamation of joy."

Lily sat in one of the hard, high-back chairs that were placed around the table they used for their various projects. "I feel terrible about this. I hope you'll manage to have fun anyway. Clara will be there, and I know how well the three of you get along."

Violet dropped into the chair next to her. "Please tell us you've changed your mind."

Violet bit her lip as she waited for Lily's reply,

and another stab of guilt went through Lily. "That is not how proposals of marriage are done. Lord Seaford asked, and I answered. I can't just invite myself to the man's home and then tell him I've changed my mind."

And especially not when she feared he would laugh in her face. But that didn't matter because, as she'd told herself countless times whenever she thought of that day one week ago, she'd made the right decision.

Violet let out a loud sigh. "I was so looking forward to this visit. Spending a few days with Clara would have been wonderful before…"

Violet didn't need to finish her sentence. *Before you ruined everything.*

"Clara is still your friend. Nothing will change that."

But now Father was going to a house party at the Seaford estate, something which he detested. And to make the entire situation worse, his sacrifice would be for naught because his daughter wasn't going to be the next countess.

When Lily refused the earl's proposal, they'd all expected that a polite excuse would be made for canceling the gathering. The Rowlands were the only guests, after all.

Instead, they'd received a short note to say that the earl was sending his carriage to collect them. After dropping off Iris, Violet, and their father at the Seaford estate, it would take Lily, alone, to the Thornton's annual Christmas house party.

Apparently Seaford hated her so much he'd gone out of his way to make it clear she was no longer welcome in his home. Her heart clenched whenever she thought about the curt note written in his slashing handwriting in black ink.

The door swung open, and they all turned to find their father standing on the threshold, his forehead furrowed in a frown.

"Are the three of you planning to stay in here forever? The carriage has arrived." He turned and strode from the room.

It would take some time for Father to forgive her. At least Iris and Violet weren't angry with her, but their misery was clear.

SEAFORD'S CARRIAGE WAS FAR MORE LUXURIOUS than their own serviceable conveyance. A small brazier was already lit, supplying just enough warmth to hold the cold weather at bay. Lily had never ridden in such comfort.

In contrast, the atmosphere within the vehicle was tense. Lily spent most of the trip looking out one of the windows while her sisters did the same. Father, however, sat there with a frown etched onto his face.

He didn't speak until they turned onto the private drive that led to the Seaford estate. "You should have told me you weren't going to accept him. It would have saved me the embarrassment of agreeing to this event."

Iris and Violet both inhaled sharply, but Father continued, turning to them. "The two of you still could have visited with Miss Howe. But there's no reason for me to be here. It's going to be damn awkward."

Lily winced as he said the last words. His harsh language was a testament to just how upset he was. Father never swore in their presence.

She looked away, unable to think of anything she could say to explain her reasoning. She'd had reservations about Seaford's courtship for some time and had even spoken to her cousin Celia about them. She could hardly tell her father that she couldn't accept Seaford's proposal because their courtship had been far too proper. She couldn't admit that she wanted to be swept off her feet. Potentially even have the man try to seduce her. At the very least, he should have tried to kiss her after six months of courtship.

She tried not to think about Celia's warning that Seaford had a reputation for being a rake. That only made his propriety worse. She couldn't help but believe he'd settled on her as a suitable candidate to be his wife but that he didn't actually *want* her.

The carriage drew to a halt, and a footman opened the door. Although she wasn't staying, Lily exited the vehicle as well. Ignoring the heavy weight that had settled in the pit of her stomach, she turned to greet the family.

Clara was Seaford's only sibling, and she rushed forward to hug Violet, then Iris, and finally Lily. The dowager countess smiled fondly at her daughter's happiness before greeting them all.

"My son sends his apologies," she said, her mouth turning down slightly. "He's had to return to London and isn't currently in residence."

She then turned to Lily and clasped one of her hands between hers. "I was sorry to hear you'd already promised your cousin you'd be joining them again this year. We were looking forward to having you here. It would have given me time to get to know you better and no doubt would have served as an inducement for my son to remain in Berkshire."

Lily was speechless for several seconds before finally murmuring something about being disappointed she couldn't join them this year.

It was clear Lady Seaford didn't know what had happened between Lily and her son. She didn't know that Seaford had already proposed and been refused.

For one moment, her heart soared as she thought that perhaps he hadn't given up on her. But then Lily chided herself for continuing to spin fantasy scenarios that were never going to take place.

If Seaford wanted another chance to woo her, he wouldn't have returned to London. And the fact that he'd personally made arrangements for her to spend this period before Christmas at the Thornton estate meant he didn't want her under his roof at all. That was the action of a man who wanted no connection between her and his family.

She stood off to the side as the trunks were unloaded. Then, after only a few minutes, it was time to say her goodbyes to everyone.

Lady Seaford turned to her. "We're sending along another servant who will ride outside with the driver. The roads between here and the Thornton estate are safe, and the journey isn't a long one, but we wanted to put your mind at ease. It's never easy to travel alone."

Lily hugged her sisters and Clara, then dipped into a curtsy before Lady Seaford.

When she turned to her father, she didn't expect to see the compassion on his face. He understood the import of the earl's actions—Lily was banished from the house. Over the years, she'd spent much time here, but those days were now at an end. Soon Lady Seaford would learn that Lily would never be her daughter-in-law.

Tears pricked at her eyes as a footman helped her into the carriage, but Lily refused to let them fall. She'd made her decision and now must live with the consequences.

She took a deep breath before pasting on a smile and turning to wave goodbye through the window.

Everything would work out in the end. Her disappointment was temporary and soon she'd be able to put it behind her. At least she could console herself with the fact that her actions hadn't cost Iris and Violet their friendship with Clara. And one day, when Seaford wed, he would no longer care about her at all and she'd be able to visit as well.

A sharp stab of pain threatened to steal her breath at the thought of Seaford marrying another woman. With great difficulty, she leaned back against the plush cushions and tried to think of something—anything—other than Seaford's future countess.

They traveled for some time before Lily opened her eyes again and gazed outside at the passing scenery. She'd hoped to find solace in sleep, but her morose thoughts refused to leave her.

She frowned when she didn't recognize the road. Where were they? It stood to reason that she wouldn't recognize this road. She'd never made the trip to the Thornton estate from anywhere other than her own home. Still, they should be approaching the manse soon. The estate wasn't that far from Seaford's.

She was about to tap on the roof to ask how much longer it would be until they reached their destination but hesitated. Instead, she cried out when they jolted to a halt. Another glance outside the window told her that they definitely hadn't reached the Thornton estate.

"Why have we stopped?" she called out, worried they might have gone over a rut in the road that damaged the carriage.

The door was flung open, and a dark figure blocked out the light. The sun was behind the man, so she couldn't tell if this was the driver or the man accompanying them to ensure her safety.

She realized it was neither when the man pulled out a pistol and aimed it at her.

CHAPTER 4

Anticipation surged through Simon's veins. The plans he'd carefully set in motion were now underway. There was no doubt in his mind that he shouldn't be so excited about his course of action, but it was time he started behaving true to form again.

Lily said she wanted passion, and he was going to show her she could have that with him. Acting the part of a gentleman hadn't won her hand, so now he would show her who he was. She needed to see that he'd been playing a role for the past six months.

He wasn't meek when it came to women. He let them know exactly what he wanted from them, and for the most part, they were more than willing to go along with whatever he suggested.

But Lily was a maiden and younger than him by eight years. Granted, he wouldn't be thirty for three more years, so he wasn't exactly old, but he had never been with someone younger than twenty. Normally his dalliances were with women his age or a little older. It was surprising how many widows were not yet thirty, but given the penchant of older men to wed women who were barely out of the schoolroom, he supposed it was to be expected. He'd had a mistress a few years ago but got tired of even that level of commitment.

Which was why he'd been shaken to realize that he didn't just want Lily in his bed, but he wanted to keep her at his side. Ensure that she was his alone.

When he'd inherited his title a few years ago, after his father had suffered an apoplexy, he'd known he couldn't put off marriage forever. But he hadn't felt the need to find a bride just yet. Whenever he did think about marrying, he'd assumed it would be to someone older, more experienced in the ways of lovemaking. Someone who could hold his interest long term.

Lily had taken him by surprise, and he couldn't say why she'd captured his interest so thoroughly.

Perhaps some part of him had recognized the hidden depths of her personality, the side of her that craved passion. But because she was an innocent, he'd hidden that side of himself from her. Acted the part of what he thought a true gentleman should be.

He would have saved so much time if he'd been himself.

He'd have to find some way to reward his valet, who'd made most of the arrangements for today. Hastings had mapped out exactly how long it would take the Rowlands to reach his estate. Seaford had also asked Hastings to escort the carriage after it left his estate. Hastings had served in the British army when he was younger and could handle himself in any situation. Lily would be safe with his valet escorting her.

Hastings had also undertaken the task of convincing the carriage driver to go along with their plan. That had involved Seaford speaking to the man and explaining exactly what he planned to do. The driver had been understandably nervous about getting involved with the scheme.

Simon had given him his word that no harm would come to Miss Rowland. He didn't know exactly what Hastings had told the man, but he had the impression it was something about Miss Rowland thinking that her suitor was boring and that the earl needed to show her he was anything but boring. Neither man said as much to him, but the driver had made a comment about women who read too much wanting romantic adventures.

He pulled out his pocket watch for what seemed to be the hundredth time as he remained hidden in a small wooded area. Right on schedule, his carriage turned onto the small road that ran alongside his hiding spot.

His body surged with excitement. He'd arrived early, of course, not wanting to take any chance he'd miss the carriage. It wasn't snowing, but it was deuced cold.

He pulled his domino into place—thank heaven for masked balls—and raised the hood of his coat over his head. He didn't know where Hastings had found the garment, but it was large enough to envelop his frame. It wouldn't be obvious that it was him, especially with the hood up and his mask in place.

He had a moment of concern as the carriage came to a sudden halt. He only hoped his assessment of this young woman was correct and that she wouldn't faint or do anything that would make him feel like a monster. The last thing he wanted to do was frighten Lily.

He crossed the space to the carriage, not looking at the two men.

"Why have we stopped?" Lily called out from inside the vehicle. He took a deep breath, his pulse hammering in his ears, and flung open the carriage door. Then he pulled out the unloaded pistol he was carrying and pointed it at her.

"Get out of the carriage."

LILY'S HEART THUNDERED, AND FOR A MOMENT SHE feared she was going to faint. She took a deep breath as she tried to hold back her panic. It would do no good to succumb to hysterics.

She found it odd when the highwayman bent to pull down the carriage steps. Why would a man who'd taken up such a dishonorable profession politely step back and wait for her to exit?

She expected to see the driver and his companion standing near the front of the carriage. Her gaze careened about wildly, and then she looked up. The two men were still seated on the bench.

Surely a thief would have secured his two greatest threats before asking her to exit.

And then the unthinkable happened. The carriage began to move.

"Wait—" she called out, unwilling to believe what was happening. They were saving themselves by leaving her behind.

Thinking only that she needed to get back into that carriage, she lifted her skirts and started to run after it. She made it only two steps before the highwayman pulled her back against him. Shock raced through her as she struggled in his grasp.

"You have my word that I'm not going to hurt you." His voice was low and far too close.

She could only stare after the carriage as it disappeared from view, her stomach hollowing out with fear. "The reassurance of a brigand holds no meaning."

CHAPTER 5

He barely held back a laugh. It shouldn't have surprised him that this woman's sharp wit would assert itself now. Still, he wanted to ease her distress, so he stuffed the pistol into a coat pocket.

He loosened his hold and turned her to face him. He kept his hands on her upper arms, though. The last thing he wanted was for Lily to hurt herself while trying to flee.

She took a deep breath and then lifted her face, taking a good look at him for the first time. Her eyes roamed over his face. His hair was covered with the black hood, but the domino he wore only concealed the upper part of his face. Surely she would recognize him before he had to reveal his identity.

After several seconds, her eyes narrowed, a slight crease forming between her brows. He wanted to drop a kiss on that line.

"Do we… know one another?"

"Why don't you find out?"

He released one of her arms and waited to see what she would do. She took another deep, shuddering breath before reaching for his face with a hand that was, thankfully, steady. How he wanted her to caress him with that hand, but that would have to wait for another time.

Lily pushed back the hood and then raised the domino to his forehead. Her eyes widened, and she sucked in a breath.

"Seaford?"

He couldn't hold back his grin. "Were you expecting someone else?"

"What…? How…?" She stamped a foot and tugged on the arm he still held. He released her, hoping she would no longer feel the need to run away from him.

"What is the meaning of this? Your mother said you were in London."

"You wanted passion, Lily." It was the first time he'd called her by her given name, and her small inhalation told him she'd taken note of that fact.

"I'm going to show you that I can give you everything you want and more."

Enjoying the way her mouth dropped open, he bent and swept her into his arms. She flung her hands around his neck but said nothing.

He kept his eyes on the path ahead, refusing to be distracted by her weight in his arms and the feel of her soft curves pressing against him.

When he reached the group of trees behind which he'd left his horse, he lowered her to her feet again. He untied the black gelding and mounted into the saddle. Realizing that the mask he'd donned was still pushed up on his forehead, he took a moment to remove it and stuffed it into a pocket. Then he leaned down and held his hand out to her.

She shook her head, her breath coming out in little puffs in the cold air. "You can't expect me to get on that horse with you."

It took a little effort to school his expression so she wouldn't see his amusement. "I'd make a poor highwayman if I went to all this trouble to gain my prize and then left her alone in the country, far away from anyone who could assist her."

Her brows drew together in a frown. She wanted to refuse him, so he continued. "It will be evening soon. And if you haven't noticed, it's starting to get colder. I think it might snow."

She let out a huff of exasperation and then placed her hand in his. "How are we going to manage this?"

Grinning, he leaned down to capture her under her arms. Ignoring the fact that his thumbs were very close to her breasts, he lifted her with ease. Again, she grasped him around his neck as he arranged her sideways on the horse in front of him. It wouldn't be comfortable for her, but they didn't have a long ride ahead.

When she didn't release her tight grasp on his neck, he leaned back slightly to look down at her. Lily's eyes were scrunched closed, her mouth pressed in a tight line. It took every ounce of strength he possessed not to try to distract her with a kiss. When he finally kissed this woman, she would want it as much as he did.

He took hold of her arms, and she allowed him to unwrap them from his neck and place them around his waist.

"Don't drop me," she said as she pressed herself closer.

"Never."

CHAPTER 6

*L*ily wouldn't swoon, but heavens, how she wanted to. She almost expected to open her eyes and discover she was dreaming.

The Earl of Seaford had kidnapped her!

Her emotions were a tangled mess as she tried to come to terms with the day's unexpected turn. She'd feared this man hated her and didn't want her anywhere near him or his family, but clearly that wasn't true.

I'm going to change your mind.

He'd said those words to her after she refused his proposal. She'd be lying if she said she hadn't hoped for something—anything—to show her that he cared for her. That he could give her the passion she craved. But a large part of her found it impossible to believe the circumspect gentleman who'd been courting her for months now would behave in such a way.

She let out a soft breath. No, he had to be playing a role, hoping to change her mind by quite literally sweeping her off her feet. And if he succeeded, it was likely he'd revert to his normal staid self.

But that didn't mean she shouldn't enjoy this little adventure while she had the opportunity.

If she was thinking logically instead of giving her romantic yearnings free rein, she would be afraid right now. But despite how much she tried to convince herself she needed to proceed with caution, she didn't believe this man would harm her.

She settled against him, enjoying the way his muscled chest felt beneath her cheek. Their position was born of practical necessity, but it was impossible not to revel in the fact that this man who had kept her at arm's length for so long was finally allowing her to get close.

She couldn't hold back her thrill of anticipation as she considered what might happen over the next few days. But if this man thought he only had to kidnap her and she would swoon at his feet, he was mistaken. If Seaford wanted her, he was going to have to win her.

Butterflies rioted in her belly at being held so intimately in Seaford's arms. Somehow, she resisted the urge to run her hands up his back. He was stronger than she'd imagined, given the way he'd easily lifted her onto the horse. She didn't think he would drop her, but she wouldn't risk distracting him.

She stayed still, enjoying the heat that emanated from his body. He'd drawn the edges of his coat over her smaller frame, and between that extra layer of wool and the man himself, she wasn't cold.

The ride wasn't long, perhaps five minutes in total, when he brought the horse to a stop. She didn't move right away, her thoughts racing as she wondered what was going to happen now.

"We've arrived, Lily." His voice was low, spoken near her ear.

He brought one hand up to her back and ran it up and down her spine. Shivers raced through her at the intimate touch. She leaned back. His brows were wrinkled in concern as he met her gaze.

Well, good. He could have frightened her to death with the events he'd set in motion today. At the very least, she could have fainted from fear.

Not that she'd ever fainted—not even when one of the stable's cats continued to bring her dead mice whenever she went riding. Iris and Violet usually asked the groom to bring their mounts outside after he'd done it the first time, but Lily knew the cat just wanted to show off his hunting prowess.

She licked her lips and noticed the way his eyes zeroed in on her mouth. "Where did you bring me?"

"Somewhere quiet where we can get to know one another."

She frowned. "I already know you, my lord."

He shook his head. "You think you know me. But that man you rejected—and rightfully so— wasn't the real me."

She should be alarmed at that statement. Her cousin's words rang in her ears again—the warning from Celia's husband that Seaford was a rake. Instead, she couldn't deny that his words had the opposite effect.

She didn't say anything as he helped her down from the horse and then swung from the saddle.

He held out his hand, and with a deep inhale, she took it. He smiled down at her before leading her and the horse to a small building that was just big enough to keep his mount safe from the elements.

She stood quietly to one side as he removed the saddle and then set about rubbing the animal down. She had to admit she enjoyed watching Seaford work. He didn't falter, and it was clear he'd done this often. She wondered how many other nobles could care for their own horses. She didn't think it was a skill that many possessed.

Finally he brought the black horse to a stall that had already been stocked with feed. He rubbed the animal's nose and whispered words of praise when the horse leaned into his touch. Lily couldn't stop remembering how good it had felt when he'd rubbed that same hand along her spine only minutes before.

Heat rose in her cheeks, and she turned away, knowing that Seaford's attention would soon be returning to her. If there was a small building for stabling a horse here, there would also be a dwelling. Which meant there would be servants even if there was no groom.

The knowledge that there would be witnesses to her current situation, more than anything else that had happened today, had her cringing with embarrassment.

CHAPTER 7

After seeing to his horse, Simon led the way to the small cottage that was tucked away in a wooded area near the edge of his Berkshire estate. At one time it was used as a hunting box, but that was before he'd purchased the estate for his mother, who had grown up in the area.

His valet had made the arrangements to have it cleaned and stocked for a short stay. Hastings had used the excuse that Seaford liked to get away for a few days of outdoor exercise and that it should always be kept ready for his use.

Their stay here wouldn't be long. He couldn't keep Lily hidden away in the country indefinitely even though the thought was appealing. When her family returned home a few days from now, they would expect Lily to also be on her way.

He'd almost reached the small stone cottage when he noticed Lily was no longer following him. He turned to find she'd halted several feet away and was gazing at the house with a hint of alarm. Her hands were clasping her upper arms, and she was shivering.

"You should come in; you're cold. There's a fire in the main room, and I can assure you it's much warmer inside than it is out here."

She bit her lower lip, her eyes fixed on the house. "Who else lives here?"

"No one. This cottage is still on my property."

She shook her head. "I mean the servants," she said, keeping her voice low. "Who will know that I'm here, alone with you?"

He crossed the space that separated them and stopped when she was within reach. He wanted to draw her into his arms to stop her shivering but restrained himself. He was getting quite good at keeping his baser instincts at bay.

"No one. It will be just you and me."

She considered his words before nodding. He held out his hand for her, but this time she didn't take it. Instead, she walked past him toward the cottage, her back ramrod straight. She stopped before the worn wooden door and turned to face him again. "What's going to happen once I cross that threshold?"

He met her gaze. "Nothing that you don't want to happen. But…"

She licked her lips, and he wanted to groan. "But?"

He was long past pretending to be circumspect with this woman. "I'm hoping I'll be able to give you *everything.*"

She swallowed visibly and stepped aside. He opened the door and again held out his hand. When she placed her hand in his, he tightened his fingers around them and led her into the cottage.

Heat engulfed them as they stepped into the front room. It was a small building that had only two rooms on the main floor—a front room and a kitchen—and two bedrooms on the second floor.

He was glad he'd taken the time to stoke the fire before leaving to meet the carriage. It had dwindled down, so he took off his coat and hung it on one of the hooks that had been placed by the front door for just that purpose. He removed his gloves and strode to the fireplace to add more wood to the fire.

When he was satisfied it would continue to keep

the small cottage warm, he turned to face Lily. He'd been slow and careful with her, knowing that he needed to give her time to get used to the situation in which she now found herself. He wasn't surprised to see she'd found the pistol he'd tucked away into one of the pockets of the voluminous coat and now stood with it pointed at him. Lily was clever, which was one of the things he'd always liked about her. She wasn't going to allow this opportunity to pass.

"You're going to take me to the Thornton estate. They're expecting me and will be worried when I don't arrive."

He took a step toward her. "No one is expecting you, Lily."

It only took her a moment to realize the truth. "Of course not. That was a lie. A way to get me away from my family so they wouldn't worry about me when you…" The pistol began to lower, but then she squared her shoulders and raised it again. "It doesn't matter. You can take me to see my cousin Celia or return me to your estate. Given the circumstances, I don't think you can continue to banish me from your home."

It was time for him to show her his hand. "I want you to be my countess and mistress of all my houses. I apologize for making you believe I didn't want you there, but it was necessary to carry out the task at hand."

Her mouth firmed into a thin line before she spoke. "The task of kidnapping me."

He took another step closer.

"Stay where you are." Her hand shook, and for a moment he wondered if she would pull the trigger.

"We only have one horse, my dear. How can I take you anywhere if I don't come near you?"

Her nose scrunched as she considered his words. Finally she let out a soft huff and lowered the pistol.

He closed the space between them and took the weapon from her hands. Then he pointed it at the ceiling and pulled the trigger.

Nothing happened.

"You… you…," she sputtered as she tried to think of an accusation to level at him.

He raised a hand and ran the back of a finger along her jaw. "It was never loaded, Lily. Did you think I would take a chance with anything that might harm you?"

She was silent for several moments. "Honestly? No. But I also never thought you'd do something like this."

A pang of guilt hit him square in the chest. "You have driven me to take desperate action."

She shook her head. "If anyone learns that the two of us were alone here together, I will be ruined." She frowned. "Is that what you're planning to do? Cause a scandal and force my hand?"

She was gazing up at him, her eyes never leaving his. As though she were trying to read his thoughts.

"I would never force you to do anything you don't want to do, and that includes marrying me." He stepped closer and leaned down so his face was inches from hers. "I give you fair warning that I will try to seduce you. But it is *you* who will have the final say in anything that happens between us."

She swallowed visibly and leaned closer to him. He didn't think she'd done so consciously, and he was tempted to act on the unspoken invitation. But not yet. It was too soon.

He dropped his hand from her cheek and took a step back. Her small pout of disappointment was gratifying.

"If you're hungry, there is food in the kitchen. But I'm afraid my skills there only go as far as setting out a cold meal that someone else has prepared."

Her head tilted to one side. "Please tell me there's tea."

"If not, someone on my staff will receive a stern reprimand."

Her smile lifted his heart, and together they made their way to the kitchen.

CHAPTER 8

*L*ily watched him as he set about unpacking the small picnic basket that had been left for them, spreading the wrapped packages of food on the small square table.

He darted a quick look her way. "Are you going to make the tea?"

"I was waiting to see if you would need help."

He crossed over to a cupboard and looked inside. "I found the plates and cutlery, so I think I'll be able to manage this."

With a small shake of her head, she turned and set the water to heat. As she prepared the kettle, her thoughts went over the events of the day. She no longer believed she was dreaming. Her imagination would never have been able to dream up the current situation in which she found herself.

She'd enjoyed sneaking into the kitchen to watch the staff go about their duties when she was younger and she knew what to do. It didn't hurt that their matronly cook would gift her with biscuits so she visited often.

She couldn't help but wonder if Seaford truly believed they could spend the next few days here alone. He was an earl and had several estates filled with servants who saw to his every need. It wouldn't take long for him to tire of cold meals.

She was so deep into her musings that she didn't notice Seaford had finished and was now watching her. When she turned back to the table after the tea was ready, he was leaning against a wall, his arms folded across his chest. His gaze was lowered—had he been staring at her backside? There was a look on his face that she'd never seen before, one that had her heart beginning to race.

His eyes rose to meet hers. He had the audacity to shrug as though he'd done nothing more than sneak into the kitchens to have a taste of the dessert that was going to be served with dinner.

Deciding that the best course of action was to

ignore the subject altogether, she brought the kettle to the table. He'd done a good job setting out the dinnerware and cutlery. A variety of cold meats, cheeses and bread were unpacked onto serving platters.

He moved behind her and held out her chair, unconcerned that he was taking on the role of a footman. Without a word she sank into it, her legs now a little unsteady, and waited for him to take the chair across the table.

When he was settled, she busied herself with pouring their tea, a sudden shyness settling over her. She already knew he took his without milk or sugar. After she passed him his cup, he waited for her to prepare her plate before doing the same.

"Do you think we'll have snow before Christmas?"

She couldn't help it, she burst out laughing. The entire situation was so ridiculous. This man had kidnapped her, spirited her away to a tiny cottage where it would be just the two of them without even one servant, and now he was talking about the weather?

His laughter joined hers, and she realized he'd been hoping to ease the tension between them with humor. It had worked.

"You didn't bring me here to exchange social niceties with me, my lord."

The corners of his mouth were still turned up in a fond smile, but there was heat in his eyes. Before today she'd caught glimpses of that, look but he'd always been quick to hide it. So quick that she thought she'd been imagining it. But in that moment, he was no longer trying to hide what he was feeling.

"We have time to talk about that later. I don't want to overwhelm you on the first night."

The way his voice dropped on the word *night* caused a shiver to run through her.

They spoke very little throughout the meal. She ignored that logical inner voice that told her she should be pressing him for details about what he was hoping to accomplish with this whole scheme. Because he was right in thinking she wasn't ready to have this conversation with him. Her thoughts and emotions were all in a jumble, and she needed a little bit of time to fully absorb everything that had happened.

When they'd finished eating, they moved in sync and began to pack away the food that remained. She washed their dishes and was shocked when he joined in to help her dry and put them away.

That task done, she turned to face him.

"I'll be back in a moment," he said before snatching up the basket and striding from the room. He opened the cottage's main door and stepped outside.

She clasped her hands at her waist, curious about what he was doing. He returned a minute later with a trunk. Her trunk.

She shook her head. Of course it was. This man had planned everything with care, so it wasn't hard to believe he'd also arranged for her belongings to be brought to the cottage.

She followed him upstairs, bemused by the fact that the so-very-proper earl she'd come to know had morphed into this man who now seemed to be a stranger.

He walked into one of the two bedrooms on the second floor and placed the small trunk on the floor. Lily hadn't packed many belongings since she was only supposed to be gone for three days.

She stayed in the hallway, nervous about being alone with Seaford in a bedroom. This man had never even kissed her, so she imagined she'd be safe with him, but there were some boundaries she wasn't yet ready to cross. Perhaps that would change by the end of their time together.

Heat rose to her cheeks as she thought about all the things that might change before she returned home.

She expected Seaford to say good night and leave her, but instead, he joined her in the hallway. He raised one hand and placed his fingers, still cold from his time outside, on her chin.

"I'm giving you fair warning, Lily. I won't do anything that you don't want me to do, but I do plan to do everything in my power to seduce you."

She didn't know what to say to that and so said nothing as their gazes held for what seemed an eternity. When his eyes lowered to her mouth, she knew what he wanted before he spoke.

"I'm going to kiss you. If you don't want that, tell me."

Now that this moment was here, Lily found that she didn't need to summon the bravery she thought she'd need. She'd wanted Seaford to kiss her so many times over the past few months, and a thrill of anticipation went through her. She'd been longing for more than friendship with this man and had feared it would never come to pass.

She licked her lips and couldn't help but notice the way his eyes narrowed on that small movement. "Yes."

He needed no further prodding. He lowered his head, and finally his mouth settled on hers. Soft and sweet, his lips brushed over hers. She exhaled a soft breath. This was nice.

His hands cupped her cheeks, and she reached at the same time for his upper arms. Not because she wanted to push him away but because she wanted to keep him close.

The press of his mouth became firmer, and then his tongue darted out to trace along the seam of her lips. She opened her mouth for him without prodding, knowing that this was how people kissed and wanting very much to experience it.

With a soft groan, he took the invitation, and his tongue swept into her mouth.

She'd never kissed a man before and thought she wouldn't know what to do. But some instinct had her mirroring his movements, allowing this kiss to go further than she knew he'd intended.

Fire coursed through her body as she realized she would give this man anything he wanted. He need only ask for it.

And then, before she was ready, it was over. He raised his head, and they stared at one another, their breathing labored.

"I'm going to stop now while I still can. We'll

have time enough to get to know one another better tomorrow."

He turned and, without looking back at her, made his way to the stairs.

She watched him as he descended. With a sigh of contentment, she entered the bedroom and closed the door. She leaned against it, her mouth widening in a grin.

She'd been expecting to spend the next few days alone with her cousin and all the guests who would be at the Thornton's house party. She knew Celia would go out of her way to make the visit an enjoyable one, but she'd been dreading it.

But instead of spending the next few days as an outcast from her family and from Seaford's, everything was bright and new.

The future held a world of promise.

CHAPTER 9

When Lily opened her eyes the next morning, it took her a moment to remember where she was. Her bedroom walls weren't yellow, and the morning sun didn't stream through her tall windows at home.

Then yesterday's events came crashing back to her.

Trying not to think about the fact that the carriage driver and the man who'd accompanied him knew she was here, alone with Seaford, she threw back the blankets and rose from the bed. She'd have to trust he'd chosen his accomplices wisely and that no one else would learn he'd kidnapped her.

Because at some point during the night she'd decided she was going to embrace this adventure with both hands. If Seaford was the proper, emotionless gentleman she'd thought him, he would have moved on and chosen another woman to court. Instead, he'd chosen to show her that he was more than capable of giving her what she craved.

Eager to see what would happen today, Lily moved to where her trunk was lying open at the foot of her bed. She hadn't unpacked it last night when she'd taken out her nightgown, but she did so now. She hung her dresses in the wardrobe that was standing in one corner of the room and placed everything else in the dresser.

With that task behind her, she chose a bright yellow dress to wear today—noting with a smile that it matched the walls of her bedroom. She'd anticipated having to share a maid with several other guests, as she'd done last year when she and her sisters had attended the Thornton house party. With that in mind, she'd selected dresses that didn't button up the back.

Grateful her foresight meant she'd be able to dress herself without the assistance of a maid, she set about preparing for the day ahead.

She sighed as she stood before the mirror. There

would be no fancy hairstyle today. She undid the plaits she normally wore when she went to bed and swept her hair up into a serviceable style.

She considered adding one of the hair combs she'd brought with her, but in the end decided against it. The earl had seen her dressed up for his visits. If he was earnest about wanting to marry her, he should know what she looked like when she wasn't going out of her way to impress others. She knew that most women would call her a fool for thinking that, but she saw it as yet another small test of Seaford's character.

Trying to tamp down the excitement that was beginning to grow within her, she made her way downstairs.

Only to find the front room and kitchen empty.

She shook her head and tried to push aside her disappointment. The earl would have to wake up at some point. Until then, she could make herself a pot of tea.

That task complete a few minutes later, she was about to prepare a cup when the unmistakable sound of the front door opening, then closing, almost caused her to drop the teacup.

She turned to the kitchen door, hoping it was Seaford who'd gone outside. But if it wasn't, she couldn't hide. The stairs were in the front room, and there was no other door in the kitchen.

She listened to the sounds of someone moving around in the other room and sent up a silent prayer that it wasn't one of the men who knew about her presence here. She wouldn't be able to face them.

She let out her breath when Seaford stepped into the doorway.

His gaze raked over her form, and she held herself still under his appraisal. This was her, Lily, without the usual finery.

She took the opportunity to appraise him as well. He wore buff-colored trousers and a simple dark blue waistcoat, but he wasn't wearing his customary topcoat. And his jaw had the beginnings of a beard which should have made him appear unkempt but somehow only accentuated the line of his jaw in a most becoming way.

When she met his gaze, he was grinning at her. The moment stretched taut between them before he broke the silence.

"I see you've made tea. Bless you."

He raised his arm to show her the basket that contained the remains of their meal from the night before. He must have kept it outside so the cold air would keep the food from spoiling.

"Did we leave enough to eat today?"

He shook his head. "I'm afraid not, but my valet dropped off another picnic basket for us."

She winced. "How many people know I'm here with you?"

"Just him and the carriage driver," he said, moving farther into the room and beginning to unpack their morning meal. "I was outside caring for my horse when he stopped by. I've been assured there is enough food to last us the rest of the day."

She brought the teapot to the table and then helped him to set out the plates and cutlery. She supposed it made sense that Seaford's personal servant was the man who'd joined them yesterday. If the earl knew the man well, that would explain why he was confident he could be trusted.

Like yesterday, Seaford helped her into the chair, and she poured their tea.

She cut thick slices of still-warm bread for the two of them and slathered a good amount of fresh butter on hers. Normally she liked toast and eggs for breakfast, but she wouldn't complain. Seaford was going to a great deal of trouble to see to their needs while also ensuring their privacy.

She took a bite, watching the way Seaford devoured his own bread and cut himself another slice. "So tell me about this cottage. Have you kidnapped any other women and brought them here?"

His grin held a hint of wickedness as he added jam to his second slice. "Only you," he said with a wink.

She took a sip of her tea as she continued to watch him. "That makes sense since you normally live at one of your other estates. So do you have one of these cottages on your other properties? Some-where to take the women you spirit away?"

He leaned back in his chair, arms crossed over his chest, and leveled a direct stare at her. "You are the only woman I've found to be worth the effort."

He spoke with such conviction, no hint of prevarication in his expression. She was sure others would think her foolish, but she believed him. Her throat went dry as he continued to stare at her, and she had to take another sip of her tea before she could continue. "I'm sure every other woman you've wanted fell at your feet."

He didn't move, and she was powerless to look away from him. "I'm no saint, Lily. And many would say I'm no gentleman. But I made sure that any woman who came before you understood that our time together would be brief. I haven't misled anyone."

"Not even me?" Her voice was barely above a whisper.

He winced. "Our whole courtship was a charade. I wanted to sweep you away that first day I met you when you'd come with your sisters to visit Clara in London."

A shiver went through her at the vehemence in his words. "But you didn't."

"No. Instead, I decided that since you were a properly bred young woman, I needed to court you. For the past few months, I've been pretending to be someone I'm not."

She sucked in a breath, shocked that he would admit as much to her. "So all those things you told me… the books you enjoy reading, your love of horses, and… everything." They'd spoken about so much. His plans to improve one of his estates, what he liked to do in his free time.

"Oh, that was all true. But I didn't want to shock you with the strength of how much I wanted you. Not to mention the fact that your father would have barred me from the house if he even suspected."

He drained the rest of his tea, and she couldn't help but wonder if he also found his throat was dry. When she caught herself watching his mouth, remembering how he had kissed her yesterday, she had to force herself to look away.

Everything about this man—his demeanor, the way he looked at her—was so different from the man she'd come to know.

Better, an inner voice said.

She'd liked him well enough before he'd abducted her. Heaven knew the man drew every female eye whenever he walked into a room—hers included. But she'd always had the feeling that he was too polite. Too considerate in how he treated her, if that was even possible. Despite that, she'd yearned for more from him, unable to shake the certainty that there was a side to this man that he wasn't showing her.

She'd feared it was because he didn't actually care for her. That he'd decided to court her because they got along well, and he saw her as a friend who would make an acceptable wife. To learn that Seaford had been hiding just how much he wanted her... Her mouth turned up in a grin as the reality of the situation hit her. She was about to get everything she'd ever wanted. The future she'd been too scared to dream about for fear she'd end up disappointed.

She looked at him again and found he was still watching her. She took a deep breath and spoke the words that would change her life forever. "I want you to show me."

CHAPTER 10

Somehow, Simon kept from jumping out of his chair. He wanted nothing more than to grab this woman and take her upstairs. But this was Lily, and he needed to make sure he wasn't misconstruing her words. There could be no more misunderstandings between them.

"I need to be certain what it is you would like me to show you." When he noticed his hands were actually shaking, he settled them palms down on top of the table and took a steadying breath before continuing. "More kisses?"

She bit her lip and nodded, and he wanted to groan. He didn't think he could touch this woman again and not ravish her.

"Also…"

The word, spoken softly, rocketed through him. "I think you know what it is I want from you. With you. But I need to know that you want it as well."

She took a deep breath and squared her shoulders. "I want you to make love to me."

He didn't leap from the table, not quite, but his chair did scrape against the floor as he pushed it back and stood. Then he stalked around the table—there could be no other word for it—and held his hand out to Lily.

She grasped it without hesitation, and he pulled her up. Then he kissed her.

This time he didn't need to start slowly, nor did he need to keep a respectable distance between their bodies so he wouldn't get carried away. Because this time they wouldn't stop.

He pulled her against him, heat flooding through him at the sensation of this woman's soft body pressed against his harder one, and caught her mouth in a kiss meant to convey just how much he wanted her. As his tongue surged into her warmth, one small part of him urged caution because even though she had consented, Lily was still a maiden.

But it was impossible to heed that warning

when Lily opened for him and returned his kiss with equal fervor. Her fingers were in his hair as she held his head close.

Without conscious thought, his hands moved from her waist to her hips and he brought her soft belly against his hardness. If he didn't pull away now, he was going to have this woman right here on the kitchen table, and Lily deserved so much more than that.

Ending their kiss was one of the hardest things he'd ever had to do. He managed it only because he knew this wasn't the end. He bent his knees and swept her into his arms again as he'd done when playing the role of highwayman.

As she did that other time, she grasped him about the neck. But this time, instead of sputtering in indignation, she laughed with joy. That sound had him believing he could do anything in the world.

He carried her upstairs, careful not to bump her into the wall or the banister on the narrow stairs. Which meant, of course, that his back grazed the wall, but he didn't mind. The only thing that mattered right then was Lily.

When they stopped in front of her bedroom

door, she reached down to turn the handle. He entered the room and strode to the bed. Then stopped.

He smiled as he looked down at it. "You made the bed?"

"Of course. I don't have a maid here to do it for me. But the sheets aren't tucked in as tightly as they should be." A small vee had formed between her brows at the admission.

He could only shake his head in amusement. He intended to keep the bedsheets in complete disarray over the next few days. How many times would she try to make the bed while he did everything in his power to muss it up again?

He wasn't sure how good the mattress springs were, so he laid her down carefully on top of the smoothed-out linens and stared down at her.

After a few seconds, she squirmed in discomfort. Red tinged her cheeks. "Either you're joining me here or I'm going to stand up right now."

That had him lowering himself to sit on the bed next to her. He took one of her hands and dropped a kiss in the middle of her palm. "I must say you've turned out to be a delightful surprise."

She let out a soft laugh. "I think your impression of *properly bred* young women is entirely too old-fashioned. I can assure you that while many young women may not approve of being kidnapped, we do long to have someone sweep us off our feet."

"And instead, I decided to plod along like a snail."

She tugged him onto the bed next to her. "You made up for it in the end in spectacular fashion."

He'd been off his game for months now, but this he knew how to do. And if he didn't ruin things again, this time they would both be winners.

She brought her hands up to his face, running her thumbs along his cheeks. "I like the way your whiskers feel."

With a grin, he dropped a kiss on her mouth and then brought his face to her neck, where he dragged his stubble against the delicate skin there. He'd have to be careful not to mark her where others might see it after they left the cottage, but he enjoyed the soft sound she made at the rasp of his whiskers against her skin.

Which of course had him thinking of doing the same thing against her breasts and the skin of her inner thighs.

The thought had him hard as a rock, and he took her mouth again. He would have to find the strength to go slow. Not too slow—he'd already learned his lesson there—but he didn't want to go too far in the other direction and scare her away.

He dragged his mouth along her jaw, kissing her just under her ear as he brought his hands to her waist. When she clasped him about the shoulders, her eager movements telling him that she enjoyed what he was doing to her, he cupped her breasts.

Her gasp of pleasure echoed his own groan. He stared down at her, enjoying the way her head was thrown back, her lower lip held between her teeth.

He traced her nipples. "Are you fine with me touching you here?"

She nodded, and he tugged down the bodice of her gown. Her eyes flew open, but she didn't protest.

Thank the heavens that she wasn't wearing stays. He palmed her through her chemise and then dropped his head to draw one rosy tip into his mouth through the fabric.

Her hands had moved to the back of his head and she held him in place.

As though he would ever want to be anywhere else.

He pushed her onto her back and switched his attention to the other breast. Emboldened by her enjoyment, he pulled down her chemise and then brought her soft breast into his mouth.

His blood heated at the small gasps of pleasure that escaped her throat. These weren't the practiced moans of a woman who was playing a role for him. He'd always taken great care when seeing to a woman's pleasure before taking his own, but he'd be a fool not to know that many of those women went to almost comical lengths to show their appreciation.

But not Lily. Her gasps were soft, as though she was surprised but nonetheless delighted by the fact she was enjoying his attention very much. There was nothing false or exaggerated about her cries.

Which had him aching to bring her to heights she could never have imagined.

He lifted his head and hovered over her. He knew this would end in him taking her maidenhead, but before that happened, he needed her to find release. He wasn't sure if she'd be able to do that with him inside her this first time.

She opened her eyes, and they stared at one another.

"Are we going to make love now?" Her voice was lower than normal, husky from her passion.

"Soon, my love. But first I need to prepare you. Your first time will hurt."

She licked her lips. "I know."

He kissed her and used one hand to drag up the skirts of her dress. She gasped into his mouth when he skimmed a hand along the delicate skin of her inner thigh, but she didn't stop him. When he reached that sweet place between her thighs, she shifted her head to one side and clenched her jaw.

He stilled. "Am I hurting you?"

She shook her head. "I'm getting ready for the pain."

He chuckled. "Not yet, Lily. First there is only pleasure."

She was so wet, and he couldn't wait to make this woman his. She let out a shuddering breath when he entered her with one finger, but the sound turned into another moan of enjoyment when he began to tease the sensitive bundle of nerves at the top of her opening with his thumb.

She bit her bottom lip again, and he was mesmerized as he watched the expressions that crossed her face. Every muscle in his body was stretched taut as he continued to concentrate all his attention on her pleasure, using his other hand to play with her sensitive breasts. But he kept his gaze riveted on her face, wanting to ensure he wasn't hurting her.

He didn't have to wait long before her hands tightened on his upper arms. She called out his name, and then the most glorious expression crossed her face as her release swept through her.

He stilled, then removed his hand and braced himself over her. Lily's eyes were wide with wonder.

"I never imagined…" She shook her head. "I was told that lovemaking could be a wondrous experience, but I never thought I'd enjoy it that much."

Her hand cupped his cheek, and he kissed her again. This time he kept his movements slow and languorous, needing to cool his own raging desire. He wanted to sink into Lily and claim her forever, but it troubled him to know he would cause her pain.

"If you want to wait—"

She moved her hand to cover his mouth. "No more waiting."

He licked her hand, and she removed it with a giggle.

"You're ticklish," he said.

She frowned at him. "No."

He laughed and flipped their positions so that

she was lying on him. "I'll have to use that information to my advantage later. But for now, there's something else we need to do."

She lowered her head to kiss him but froze when a loud thumping came from downstairs.

Damn it. Someone was knocking on the front door.

CHAPTER 11

*T*he pounding of fists on the front door downstairs had the same effect as someone standing over them and throwing a basin of water onto their heated bodies.

Lily froze for several seconds as her mind tried to process what she was hearing. "Someone is here," she said in a whisper.

"They're outside." Seaford rose from the bed.

Lily scrambled up as well, pulling her chemise and dress back into place. Seaford was still fully clothed. The only sign they'd been engaged in intimacies was his hair, which was now tousled from her fingers raking through it. She knew the same couldn't be said for her.

"I'm sure it's Hastings. He must need to speak to me. I'll go see what he wants."

She nodded as she flew to the small dressing table and glanced at the mirror. Seaford had taken her hair down with only a few swift flicks of his fingers. She tried not to dwell on what that said about his experience undressing women. As for his other actions… well, if she had any doubts before, it was clear this man was no saint. Which gave credence to his assertion he'd been going out of his way to behave as a proper gentleman when he was courting her. Because it was now clear that the Earl of Seaford was not lacking in passion.

She set about twisting her hair and pinning it back onto her head. She heard the unmistakable sound of the front door opening and then the soft murmur of male voices. She took comfort in the fact that their voices weren't raised. She'd been half afraid her father had learned about Seaford's actions and had set out to track them down.

When Seaford returned a few minutes later, she was sitting on the edge of the bed. She'd managed to calm her racing heart, but her body still thrummed with heat and desire for this man. She said nothing as he crossed the room and lowered himself onto the bed next to her.

"I apologize for the interruption."

Lily winced. "It takes a little of the romance out of the situation when I'm reminded that others know we're here together and no doubt imagining what we're doing."

"Hastings will never reveal what he knows."

Lily examined his features for a hint of uncertainty, but she could see none.

"But he did come with news," he said.

Lily's breath caught. "Does Father know about us? Or perhaps something has happened to Iris or Violet—"

He cut her off with a kiss that lasted longer than it should have. It was unseemly how easily this man could distract her.

He pulled back and gazed down at her.

"Nothing like that. But your father is worried about you traveling alone. He sent a note."

She hadn't even noticed that he had a letter in his hand until he held it out to her.

She took it and broke the seal, surprised that her fingers weren't shaking. Her eyes skimmed over the page. It was just as Seaford had said—a few lines about how he was writing to make sure that she'd arrived at the Thornton estate safely. He also wanted to make sure she wasn't feeling lonely being apart from her family.

Lily almost laughed aloud at that. Seaford hadn't given her the opportunity to think about anyone but him. "Father is waiting for my reply."

Seaford nodded. "Hastings is downstairs. He took the liberty of bringing everything you'd need to write a letter."

Lily rose to her feet, her thoughts whirling as she went to the window and looked outside. Behind her, Seaford stood and she knew he was watching her. Waiting for her reply.

"I can't lie to my father."

"You wouldn't have to. You did arrive at your destination safely. And I imagine it wouldn't be a falsehood to tell him you're enjoying yourself."

She turned and smiled at him. "I am, so very much. But I need to return."

He let out a breath and closed the distance between them. "I expected you to say as much."

"Are you going to keep me here anyway?"

His brows drew together in a slight frown. "Of course not. I've already told you that I won't force you to do anything. If you wish to return to the estate, we'll do that."

She winced. "We can't return together. I must

go alone. Did your valet bring the carriage? I can leave with him now." She turned back to look at her reflection in the mirror again. "I should probably change first. My dress is a little rumpled after this morning's activities."

Heat rose to her cheeks, but she couldn't regret what had happened between them. Her only disappointment was that their time together had been so short.

Her thoughts flitted from one thing to the next as she tried to settle on what she needed to do first. What was she going to say when she returned? Seaford would want her to lie to her father about what had happened.

His large hands settled on her shoulders. She met his gaze in the dressing table mirror as he drew her back against his chest. "Breathe, Lily. We have time to talk about what is going to happen next."

He was correct. She closed her eyes and leaned back into him. When his arms wrapped around her waist, she put her own arms over them. She took comfort from the way he surrounded her body, holding her in a protective embrace.

She took several deep breaths and willed her nerves to settle. Everything would be fine. Seaford had planned this adventure with great care. So of course he would have made plans for what would come next.

A few minutes passed like that, Seaford's warmth wrapping around her. When she opened her eyes, he was watching her in the mirror. "What do we do now?"

He dropped a kiss into her hair. "You're correct that you need to change. Then I'll help you pack your belongings while Hastings fetches the carriage. He left it a little ways down the road."

She took a deep breath and nodded.

"But before we do anything else, I have something to ask you."

He removed his arms from around her waist and turned her to face him. Then he dropped to one knee.

"Lily Rowland, you've led me on a merry chase. I fumbled things badly the first time I asked, but you should know that my feelings are unchanged. Please make me the happiest of men and say that you'll agree to be my wife."

Warmth unfurled in her chest. Had it only been one week since she'd turned down this man's proposal of marriage? She'd been a fool. She opened her mouth to reply, but he held up one finger to stop her.

"You should know that I promise to fill every one of your days—and your nights—with more passion than you can imagine."

She laughed. "I'm not sure that's possible. I've been told that I have a very vivid imagination."

One corner of his mouth kicked up in a wicked grin, and her heart did a little flip in her chest. She would never get used to just how handsome this man was—and soon he was going to be hers.

"If you accept me, I'm sure I'll be up to the challenge. But I don't think I'll be able to successfully abduct you a second time if you refuse me."

She reached for his hands and tugged him back to his feet. She could only stare at him, unable to believe she'd gained this man's attention.

After several seconds, he brought her hands to his mouth and dropped a kiss onto each of her palms. "You haven't answered me."

She smiled. "No, I haven't."

His brows drew together. "I love you, Lily, and I won't give up. But I don't think I could handle another rejection from you."

Her mouth dropped open, shock rippling through her, and she had to snap it closed. "You love me?"

His brow furrowed. "Of course I do. Why would I go to all this trouble if I didn't love you?"

She gazed up at him in wonder. "I love you too. And yes, I'll marry you."

He kissed her then, quickly, and reached into a small pocket on his waistcoat. He pulled out an ornate gold ring. If she wasn't mistaken, it held a large ruby surrounded by small diamonds. "This was my parents' betrothal ring. If it doesn't fit, I can have it resized for you."

She sucked in a breath. "You didn't have this the last time you asked me."

He shook his head. "I did. I've been carrying it around with me for some time. I just didn't have the chance to give it to you the first time I proposed."

What was he saying? "You've had this the whole time?"

"I hoped you'd give me another chance to ask you again."

She placed a hand over the small pocket that was on the left side of his waistcoat, then dragged her hand to the center of his chest. "Close to your heart." Her voice was low, the significance of his actions speaking volumes.

"It's where you've been since I met you." He slid the ring onto her finger, and she was pleased to see that it fit her perfectly. As though it had been made for her.

He gathered her into his arms, and they stayed like that for several minutes. She wanted to remain there forever. Finally, far too soon for her liking, he dropped another kiss on top of her head and pulled back to look down at her. "I've already given some thought about what we're going to tell your family."

She winced at the reminder. "We can't tell them you kidnapped me and whisked me away to your secret lair."

"No. But I don't expect you to lie. To begin, we'll return together. When we arrive at the estate, I'll take your father aside. I'll tell him that I went to see you at the Thornton's house party and was able to convince you to change your mind."

It was a believable fabrication. Far more believable than the truth. And given that her father was unlikely to ask his niece and her husband for any of the details about their Christmas house party, he wouldn't learn she'd never been there.

"Perhaps I should return on my own first—"

He dropped a kiss onto her lips. "No. I'm not letting you out of my sight. Not until I've had your father's agreement and everyone knows you'll soon be the next Countess of Seaford."

"You need have no fear about that. Father might even cease being angry with me for denying you the first time."

"I was less than pleased myself, but in retrospect…" He shook his head.

She frowned. "Surely you're not glad that I refused you?"

He lifted one shoulder in a shrug. "Who knows how much longer I would have carried on pretending to be a proper suitor?" He shuddered. "And we never would have had this delightful little adventure."

"That's true," she said. She was about to say more but embarrassment had her holding her tongue.

Seaford must have seen her hesitation. "What are you thinking?"

She covered her face with her hands. After the intimacies they'd already shared, she really shouldn't be so shy around this man. Dropping her hands, she met his gaze. "That it would have been nice if your servant could have waited another few hours before delivering his message."

He pulled her against him, and she felt his hardness press into her belly. Regret filled her as she wondered whether they'd have another opportunity to be alone together before they wed.

"Make no mistake," he said into her hair. "We'll be getting to that very soon." Then he released her. "I need to go now while I still can."

With that, he strode from the room, closing the door carefully behind him.

Lily stared at the door for a few seconds and then spun in a circle, her eyes closed as she allowed pure joy to bubble through her.

Seaford loved her. It was true that they were still friends—she hadn't been wrong about that—but they were also so much more.

When she'd woken yesterday morning, the future appeared bleak. Now it promised to hold far more happiness than she could have imagined.

CHAPTER 12

Simon was relieved Lily had managed to rein in her panic after reading her father's note. Hopefully she'd be able to dress herself because he wasn't sure he'd be able to help her. Not when he wanted to do the exact opposite.

He summoned Hastings to his room to help him with his own preparations. When they arrived at his estate together, it couldn't be obvious that he'd just left Lily's bed. He needed to behave with the propriety her father expected from him.

Even if the only thing Simon wanted to do was swing the man's daughter over his shoulder and carry her to his bedroom so they could finish what they'd started.

But it seemed the fates were conspiring against him, and he'd have to wait. Again.

He took the seat next to Lily in the carriage, his heart soaring when she'd allowed him to put his arm around her and draw her to his side. Hastings had already brought his mount back to the estate last night, so he was saved from having to ride outside where he would have spent the entire trip fretting about how Lily was faring inside the carriage.

Her head rested against his shoulder, her eyes closed. But he knew Lily wasn't asleep. She would be thinking about the scandalous fact they were returning together. Unchaperoned and unwed.

He dropped a kiss into her hair. "Try not to fret. Everything will work out as it should."

They stayed like that for the half-hour trip back. When the carriage began to slow, she looked up at him, her eyes wide.

He stole a kiss from her delectable lips and then moved to the opposite bench. He knew it wasn't enough. Her father would still worry about what had happened in that carriage, especially since they were supposed to be returning from the Thornton house party, but he wouldn't flaunt their indiscretions. Not when he hoped to repeat them soon.

"Your father will be happy for us," he said.

Lily sighed. "I know. But I'm not looking forward to the lecture he'll deliver when he pulls me aside."

He should be feeling guilty about causing this woman even a moment of trouble, but he didn't. He'd do everything all over again. It had only given them one day together, but he'd achieved his goal of winning Lily's heart.

They'd discussed what would happen next. When the carriage arrived, he expected everyone's curiosity would have them coming to see who was in it.

So when he opened the carriage door and stepped down, he wasn't surprised to find their families spilling from the house to stand by the entrance. He gave Lily a reassuring smile as he helped her down from the carriage.

The group remained close to the house, not wanting to step farther out into the cold. His sister was whispering with Lily's sisters, smiles and giggles making it clear that their hopes for a wedding had been restored.

His mother gave him a chiding look as she welcomed them back, but he could tell she was doing everything in her power to hide how much she enjoyed seeing the two of them together. When he turned to look at Lily's father, he couldn't discern what the man was thinking.

"I'm so happy to see the two of you here," his mother said as everyone moved into the house. "But you must tell us how the two of you came to arrive here together."

"Yes," Mr. Rowland said, his brows drawing together. "Please share how you came to be alone in a carriage with my daughter when I was told you'd returned to London."

The hint of anger in the man's tone wasn't surprising. Seaford had expected much more.

"Of course. But first I must speak to Mr. Rowland alone."

That had their sisters gasping and then whispering again. He was relieved to see that Lily was the picture of calm.

He led her father to his study and closed the door behind them.

"I don't want to know the details," Rowland said. "Just tell me that you've managed to convince my stubborn daughter to accept your suit."

Seaford managed not to grin. "I did."

Rowland nodded. "And this happened at Thornton's Christmas party?"

He inclined his head. The lie was a necessary one, and he knew that Lily's father wouldn't go out of his way to confirm it. As Rowland had already said, he didn't want to know exactly what had happened.

"Good. I take it you'll be getting a special license?"

"I plan to leave for London first thing in the morning."

It was a week before Christmas. He'd have to call in some favors, but he was certain he could get the license this close to the holiday.

And then he'd finally have Lily, which was the best Christmas gift he could have asked for.

HE FOUND IT DIFFICULT TO HOLD ON TO HIS optimism as the day progressed. Whenever he thought he'd be able to snatch a moment alone with Lily, one of their sisters would intrude and pull her aside to join them in some activity or other. And while his mother would have looked away to allow them a few minutes together, Lily's father was not of the same mind.

Finally he gave up and headed to his study. He

didn't need anyone to tell him he'd been mooning after her like a lovesick fool. No one said as much, but he had the impression their sisters were taking an inordinate amount of pleasure in ensuring he and Lily were kept apart.

Perhaps it was what he deserved after making Lily feel that she wasn't welcome here, but he'd had enough of the glances and giggles that were aimed his way.

He tried to go over the account books, but he couldn't concentrate on numbers. Then he tried reading, but his thoughts kept straying to that morning's passionate encounter and the fact that Lily wasn't his yet.

He was pacing when a brisk knock at the study door sounded a moment before it was flung open. Clara stormed into the room and stopped in front of him. She settled her hands on her hips and scowled at him.

He let out a sigh. He didn't know why his sister was so angry with him. He was the one being thwarted at every turn. "You wished to speak to me?"

"I am very cross with you. Violet just told me that you'd already asked for Lily's hand, and you never said a word about it. And then you bungled it badly, and she refused you!"

He reached up to rub at the back of his neck, where the tension of the day had settled like a knot. "I didn't want to disappoint you and Mother."

She stamped her foot, and he had to force himself not to roll his eyes at her dramatics. "I could have helped you," she said, flinging her arms wide. "Spoken to her and tried to get her to see that you're not all that bad."

He let out a dry chuckle. "That's high praise indeed coming from you. I'm sure she would have flung herself into my arms and accepted me on the spot after learning I wasn't *all that bad.*"

"Simon." His name was a drawn-out whine.

"I already had a plan and didn't want to involve you. I would make a poor prospect for a husband if I needed to have my little sister beg a woman to accept my suit."

She crossed her arms over her chest. "I'm sixteen."

He raised one brow. "Your point?"

She let out a huff in annoyance. "Your *plan* is the other reason I'm angry with you. Why did you have to seek her out and propose again at the

Thornton's house party? You could have done it here."

He smiled. He and Lily had only spent one day together in that small cottage, but he'd always cherish the memories they'd made there. In fact, he'd make sure to visit again after they wed. Finish what had so unceremoniously been interrupted.

Clara let out an impatient huff. Then she threw herself at him and wrapped her arms around his waist. "I'm so glad you were able to fix things even if I don't approve of being kept in the dark. Lily, Iris, and Violet are like sisters to me. And now they'll be family."

He hugged her. "I'll admit I'm also relieved. Miss Rowland had me worried for a bit."

Clara pulled away. "You're forgiven. Now come along. It's almost dinner, and you shouldn't be buried away in your study. After, we're going to the music room and will take turns playing and singing. It will be so much fun. But you have to promise not to join in. We don't need your horrible singing voice ruining what will be a fun evening."

He could only shake his head as he followed Clara from the room, trying to push away the frustration that gnawed at him. He'd waited this long for Lily Rowland. Surely one more evening wouldn't kill him.

HE WAS WRONG... THE EVENING WAS GOING TO DO him in. Watching Lily as she laughed and smiled at everyone. Listening to her sing while their sisters played the pianoforte, her sweet voice wrapping around him. And the twinkle in her eyes whenever she glanced at him had him wanting to spirit her away from the room.

But her father was guarding her like a hawk. She couldn't even sit next to him, in a room filled with people, without Rowland glaring at him and inching closer so they couldn't have a private conversation.

Not that Lily's father was wrong in distrusting him. But Simon was going to be leaving for London in the morning, and he wanted at least a few minutes alone with his betrothed before then.

Finally the last song was played and the evening's entertainments were finished. Much laughter and hugs were shared as everyone said their good-nights and made their way from the room. And then it was just the three of them. Him, Lily, and Lily's father.

Rowland moved to the doorway but didn't leave. Simon wanted to growl at the man, but Lily's hand on his arm made him realize he was scowling.

"You're leaving in the morning?" she asked.

He had to keep his hands clasped behind his back so he wouldn't reach for her and drag her into his arms. He didn't care that it would anger Rowland. He was going to marry this woman, after all, and the man was unlikely to forbid the match at this late stage.

Still, he knew that angering her father would upset Lily, and that knowledge was enough to keep him on his best behavior.

"I'll be off to London for a special license. After waiting six months and having you turn me down once, I find I no longer have the patience to wait."

She smiled at him. "I agree."

She started to lean closer, and before he could reach for her and give her the kiss she clearly wanted, Lily's father was at her side. With a sigh, she waved at him over her shoulder as Rowland dragged her away.

He regretted not spiriting Lily away to Gretna Green while he had the chance.

Frustration had him stalking to his bedroom. Perhaps all was not lost. If Hastings didn't already know, he could ask the man to make discrete inquiries about where Lily was sleeping. Then, after a suitable amount of time had passed, Simon could make his way to Lily's bedroom.

His mother waylaid him for a few minutes, telling him how happy she was that he had made up with Lily. Like his sister, she also chastised him for making Lily feel as though she wasn't welcome there.

When he finally reached his bedroom, he wasn't surprised to find Hastings was already there. This man had been invaluable to him over the past week.

"Do you know where Miss Rowland is sleeping tonight?"

His valet inclined his head. "Of course. There is little that goes on under this roof that I don't know."

Simon blew out a breath. "Good. How long should I wait before I can safely make my way there?"

"It goes without saying that now would be too soon."

He frowned at the man. He knew that Hastings was trying to ease his employer's tension with humor, but the only thing Simon needed was Lily in his arms again.

Hastings bounced on his feet, and Simon didn't hold back his groan. If his valet was excited, it must mean that Hastings had ordered new clothes for him and wanted to test their fit. Simon was in no mood to indulge the man even if he did owe him a debt. "I'm not changing."

The corners of his valet's mouth turned up ever so slightly. "I do think you should look in your dressing room. I've recently *acquired* something that I think will be of great interest to you."

Simon pulled out his pocket watch and took in the time. How much longer would he have to wait before he could safely sneak through the house to his betrothed's bedroom? Perhaps it would be better to allow Hastings to dress him up in another outfit. It would allow some of that time to pass.

He turned and crossed to his dressing room. His hand was on the doorknob when he heard his bedroom door open and close. When he turned, he found he was alone in the room.

Wondering just what Hastings was playing at, he continued into the dressing room.

And found Lily standing there, waiting for him.

CHAPTER 13

"I hope I'm not intruding on your personal time."

The grin that crossed Seaford's face made her glad she'd risked coming here. She'd dismissed the maid soon after her father had deposited her at the bedroom door, telling her she wouldn't be needed. Impatience had her risking exposure, but when she'd slipped out of her bedroom, the earl's valet was waiting for her in the hallway.

She hadn't asked if the earl had sent for her or if he'd somehow read her mind and known she meant to find her way to the room Clara had once mentioned belonged to her brother. She'd allowed him to lead her here and had been amused when he'd asked her to wait in the dressing room.

Seaford opened his arms, and she threw herself at him. She loved her family and appreciated the way Clara had gone out of her way to make Lily feel as though they were already sisters. But as the hours passed and it became clear she wouldn't have another moment alone with this man, she'd known it was time to take matters into her own hands. To show Seaford that she too was willing to take a risk for him. For them.

He gave his head a small shake. "I can't believe you came here. I was doing everything in my power not to march straight to your bedroom while there was still a risk I'd be seen."

"Alas, I've never been known for my patience," she said with an exaggerated sigh. "And I didn't want to risk not seeing you again before you had to leave."

He lowered his head until his mouth hovered over hers. "That was never going to happen."

And then he kissed her, and she forgot about everything and everyone except for this man who would soon be her husband.

She let out a gasp when he swung her into his arms. "You need to warn me before you do that. I could have screamed."

He grinned down at her. "You still might."

Then he carried her from the dressing room and lowered her onto his bed. "But first, I need to lock the door so we won't be interrupted again."

She laughed. "I've already warned Mr. Hastings."

HE COULD ONLY SHAKE HIS HEAD IN SURPRISE AS HE moved to the door. It seemed that Lily had lost some of her inhibitions. He'd have to see what he could do about causing her to drop the ones that remained.

When he turned back to her, his hand was already loosening his cravat. He enjoyed the way her eyes widened as he pulled the fabric from his throat, allowing his shirt to drop open at the neck.

He made quick work of removing his waistcoat and then drew his shirt up over his head. Lily's eyes remained fixed on him the whole time, although now they lowered to his chest. When her tongue dipped out to lick her lower lip, he couldn't hold back his groan.

He made quick work of his trousers and then lowered himself to lie next to her.

Only now Lily was sitting up, her gaze traveling

up and down his body before snagging on his hard length.

"I think I'm wearing too much," she said finally.

He laughed and stretched out to allow her to look her fill. "I can lie here and watch you disrobe."

She shook her head and covered her face with her hands. "I don't think I'm ready for that. Not yet."

He would hold her to that unspoken promise, but he could work with what he had. "Kiss me, Lily."

She peeked at him through her fingers before finally dropping her hands. She took a breath, gathering her courage, and then leaned forward. When her hands remained on her lap, he laughed.

"You can touch me."

She shook her head. "I feel ridiculous."

"Never," he said, taking hold of her hands and bringing them to his chest.

Her mouth dropped open for a moment before her lips curved into a smile. Then she was exploring his chest, his shoulders, his arms. When she brought them back to his chest, she kissed him.

He tugged her down, and her breath came out in another gasp as he dragged her over his body. She let out a soft moan as he deepened the kiss, giving her a small taste of just how he wanted to devour her.

His patience at an end, he pulled down the bodice of her dress so her breasts could spring free. He rolled so she was now under him and devoured her soft flesh. Her fingers combed through his hair as she held him against her.

"You make me feel things I never imagined possible," she said, her voice ragged with desire.

He stared down at her, taking a few moments to regain control. This was her first time and it would hurt, but damn, he wanted to be inside her so much he might just die from the pressure building within him.

He'd wanted to strip her dress from her delightful body so she was as naked as him, but that would come next time. For now, he shifted onto one elbow and inched up her skirts.

"That's it," he said when she opened her legs for him.

Like last time, he used his fingers to bring her to her first orgasm. And when her body was still spasming around his fingers, her lower lip clenched between her teeth to hold back her cries, he moved into position. Ever so slowly, he inched his way into her warm, welcoming body.

Her soft gasp told him that he'd breached her maidenhead, but he didn't stop until he was seated fully within her.

It was almost impossible not to keep going. He tried counting in his head, telling himself she needed time to adjust to his invasion. He'd reached twenty when Lily shifted.

"I thought there would be more," she said.

He couldn't hold back a chuckle. By way of reply, he pulled out of her body then eased himself back in. His eyes remained fixed on her face, watching for any sign that he was hurting her.

Her soft "oh" of astonishment told him everything he needed to know. He began to move slowly then, spurred on by the way she wrapped her legs around him and arched up into his body. He had never wanted to be with a woman more than Lily, and now that he finally had her, he never wanted their time together to stop.

When she came apart, her mouth pressed against his shoulder to muffle her screams, he was right behind her.

He kissed her as his length softened inside her, and then he turned so they were on their sides, facing one another.

She reached out to twine the fingers of one

hand with his. "I can see now why Celia enjoys being with her husband so much."

He squeezed her fingers. "I hate that I must leave you tomorrow."

A small vee formed between her brows. "Must you go so soon?"

"The sooner I go, the sooner we can wed. And then nothing will keep us apart. But for now"—he rolled onto his back, and Lily nestled into his side— "we can spend some time together."

Her body needed time to heal before they could make love again, but he could at least hold her until it was time for her to return to her bedroom.

CHAPTER 14

Surely an eternity had passed since Lily had last seen Seaford. Five days. She couldn't hold back her fear that it would begin to snow and the roads would become impassable. A special license would do them no good if her betrothed couldn't reach her.

They'd said their goodbyes to Clara and Lady Seaford yesterday and were now back home. Father was the only person happy about that situation.

Seaford's mother had extended an invitation to have them stay until Christmas. Violet and Iris had tried to cajole Father to accept, but his mind wouldn't be swayed. Lily had known the effort would be futile.

Perhaps next year, when she was the new countess, they could all spend Christmas there.

Lily stood and walked over to the windows of the morning room. It was midmorning, and as was their custom, they were passing the time with various activities. Violet was scribbling away in her journal, and Iris was working on a drawing.

Lily had been trying to read. She peered out the window into their back garden. "Do you think it will snow?"

Violet let out an exasperated sigh. "Since neither one of us can predict the future, why do you insist on asking that same question twenty times a day?"

"Just twenty?" Iris said. "I'd say that number is closer to fifty."

Lily blew out a breath. Then she spotted a lone snowflake drifting on the wind, and her heart threatened to stop. She snatched up her book. "I'm going to take this to the drawing room." Where she'd be able to see an approaching horse.

"He's not going to get here any faster if you stare out a different window," Iris said.

Lily ignored her and was just about to leave the room when a knock at the front door echoed through the house. Lily dropped her book on a chair and raced down the hall, reaching the door just as the butler did.

She held her breath and waited for the man to open the door.

When it did, Seaford was standing on the threshold.

Somehow she restrained herself from pushing past their butler and throwing herself into his arms. Aware of voices behind her, she aimed for a level tone as she took a step closer. "You took longer than I expected."

His gaze was intense, and she knew, from the heat reflected in his eyes, that he was remembering the night they'd spent together.

"I reached the estate last night. Mother said she was going to ask you to stay. Imagine my disappointment when I discovered you'd all gone home."

"Are the two of you going to stand in the doorway all day?" Father said from behind her.

Lily laughed and stepped aside with an apology. She waited while Seaford handed his winter garments to the butler and was rewarded with a kiss to her cheek.

He moved to whisper into her ear. "Soon we'll be able to do much more than that."

"Not in Father's presence. I don't think he'll care how long we've been married."

Seaford raised a brow at that but said nothing, and she had the impression that he'd taken her words as a challenge. She still forgot, on occasion, that he wasn't the politely distant man who had courted her.

He tucked her hand into his arm, and together they entered the drawing room. Three sets of eyes were fixed on them.

"Well, don't keep us waiting," Father said. "Did you get what you were after?"

Seaford inclined his head, and Lily's heart lightened with relief.

He turned to her. "I took the liberty of stopping by your parish church and had a pleasant conversation with Mr. Bailey. He's agreed to marry us this afternoon."

Lily's hands flew to cover her mouth, which was gaping open most unbecomingly. "So soon?"

"Soon? We've been courting for months now."

"Your mother and your sister—"

"Are on their way. I didn't want to wait for them to get ready, so I rode on ahead."

"But—"

He placed one finger on her lips. "Have you changed your mind?"

She searched his gaze and saw that he was genuinely concerned. Of course he was. She'd already turned down his proposal once.

His finger was still on her mouth, and so she clasped his hand between hers. She dropped a kiss onto the center of his palm and then lowered it.

"Never." She let out a soft laugh of disbelief. "It appears we're getting married today. I can just imagine the rumors that will spread at our haste."

Father cleared his throat, and she dropped Seaford's hand and took a step back.

Her sisters swept forward to engulf Lily in a hug.

"At least now you won't need to spend the entire day staring out the window waiting for Lord Seaford," Violet said in a whisper that everyone in the room could hear.

Lily wasn't even embarrassed. She was far too happy for any other emotion to take up room in her heart.

"Shush," Iris said. "We're going to let the maid know that she'll be needed soon." She gave Lord Seaford a small curtsy and then dragged Violet from the room.

Lily turned to face her father. "Can I speak to Lord Seaford for a moment?"

She almost expected him to say no. Instead, he drew her into a hug. "I love you, Lily. I'm pleased this day has come."

She pulled back to stare up at him, shocked that one tear was tracing down his cheek. "I love you too, Father."

He gave his head a shake and let out a breath. "That's enough of this sentimental nonsense. We need to get the two of you married. Heaven knows this man must have the patience of a saint to have waited all this time." He shook his head again. "And Thornton told me to keep an eye on you because you were a rake."

With a silent laugh he strode from the room.

Words failed her. She stared after her father for several seconds then turned to see the scowl on Seaford's face.

"I'm going to have a few words with Thornton."

Lily stood on tiptoes and pressed a kiss onto his cheek. Seaford's arms wrapped around her as he brought her closer.

"I've missed you," she said. "Our time together was far too short."

He raised a brow. "Six months, Lily. Six months being on my best behavior when all I wanted to do was spirit you away and have my wicked way with you."

A shiver of anticipation raced down her spine. "You'll have me tonight and every night after that."

"Don't forget the days. I wouldn't want you to accuse me again of lacking in passion."

The gleam in his eyes told her she'd never have to worry about that happening.

Two days before Christmas

They were a small yet boisterous group as they spilled from the small parish church that afternoon.

Lily was tugged away from her new husband by Iris, Violet, and Clara, who engulfed her in hugs.

Seaford's mother smiled fondly before pulling her into an embrace as well. "You're good for him," she said into Lily's ear. "I'm very happy to welcome you into the family."

Father cleared his throat. "We should all return home for a pre-Christmas/very late wedding breakfast."

They all erupted into laughter, and Lily gave him a hug. "Thank you."

When the maid had helped her dress, she'd chattered nonstop about how Mr. Rowland had put the staff on alert, telling them that they were to prepare to have the wedding breakfast on a moment's notice.

Lily looked over to the side, where Seaford was speaking to his sister and mother. When Lady Seaford's hand flew to her mouth, Lily made a note to ask him what he'd said. Whatever it was, it had Clara giving her brother an exuberant hug.

Her sisters were saying something to her, but Lily could only hear her heart thundering in her ears as Seaford turned his head and met her gaze. There was an intensity in his expression that had her thinking she needed to look away for the sake of propriety.

She hoped that Mr. Bailey hadn't followed them out because her husband's wicked thoughts were laid bare on his face for the world to see. Her sisters may not understand what that look meant, but her father would.

Seaford strode across the few feet that separated them and then swung her into his arms. She gasped with shock and wrapped her arms around his neck. Her cheeks heated with color.

"What are you doing?" she hissed under her breath. "Surely you could have waited until later. What will everyone say?"

His grin was full of wicked promise as he turned and strode toward the two carriages they'd taken to the church. "They'll say that I didn't have the decency to wait until after the wedding breakfast, but instead carried you off to my lair with unseemly haste."

Her mouth dropped open before she snapped it closed again. "What... lair?"

"Yes, my love. I'm abducting you. And I have the perfect little cottage waiting for us."

"But our families—"

He dropped a kiss onto her mouth. "My mother and sister know not to expect us. I have other plans for you."

And that was how Lily Rowland, now the new Countess of Seaford, was said to have received a highwayman for Christmas that year.

A ROGUE FOR CHRISTMAS

CHRISTMAS SCANDALS

BOOK 3

If he was a better man, he'd stay far away from Iris Rowland. But no one had ever accused the Earl of Wentworth of being a good man.

After saving Iris from certain ruin, the unthinkable happens. He becomes obsessed with the memory of the young woman he rescued at the end of the season.

There is only one thing to do. Secure an invitation to the Christmas house party she'll be attending. But instead of putting his curiosity about Iris to rest, he is shocked to discover that his inconvenient attraction might be something more.

CHAPTER 1

December 1818

If he were a better man, he'd stay far away from Miss Iris Rowland. But no one had ever accused the Earl of Wentworth of being a good man. Which was why he'd gone out of his way to secure an invitation to Viscount Thornton's annual Christmas house party.

It was a calculated risk since he couldn't be certain Iris would be in attendance. But his discreet inquiries had shown this was his best course of action. His only path forward, really, if he didn't want to wait until the next season began before he could see her again.

It had been years since Wentworth had ventured into the country for Christmas. Normally he spent the day in London, where he wouldn't have to listen to his mother's constant lectures about his unbecoming conduct. Staying in town also made it easier to conduct his affairs.

Not that he'd engaged in any liaisons of late, which was precisely the reason he was in Surrey. Iris Rowland was constantly in his thoughts—he'd even dreamed about her. Drastic action was needed to exorcise whatever spell she'd cast over him.

He'd only spoken to her once, and their encounter had been brief, but every second of their meeting out in the gardens during the last ball of the season was etched in his memory.

He'd grown bored early in the evening and made arrangements to meet an overeager new widow for a bit of fun. He'd been finding it increasingly difficult to enjoy his customary amusements of late and feared he was growing jaded. Hoping it was only a phase, he slipped out into the dimly lit gardens.

The moon wasn't positioned correctly to supply enough light that evening, and the large shrubs and flowering bushes cast dark shadows along the path.

But light wasn't a requirement for what would happen tonight. One body was very much like another in the dark.

He blamed the shadows for his error in mistaking the woman standing in the garden for the buxom widow.

She was already waiting for him, facing away. He let out a sigh as he moved into place behind her. She was too old to make the mistake of turning her back on the path, where anyone could come across her.

He placed his arms on her hips and dragged her back into him. His mouth was already dropping to the exposed expanse of skin at the base of her neck when the unexpected happened. She raised her arm, but instead of reaching back to bury her fingers in his hair, she brought her elbow back sharply against his midsection.

It wasn't enough to hurt him, of course, but he released her at once. He enjoyed his dalliances, but he would never force a woman. Seduce her, yes, but he'd never use force. He was also annoyed that she was playing games with him. If this woman thought that he was going to chase her to get what he wanted, she would be sorely disappointed.

He was preparing to tell her just that as she spun around to face him, but the admonition died on his lips.

Dammit, this wasn't the eager widow from the ballroom. No, the indignant young woman was the last person he'd expected to find here.

Iris Rowland. Sister-in-law to the Earl of Seaford and, from all indications, an innocent.

He watched the play of emotions cross her lovely face. Indignation, then shock. Her blue eyes widened, and her hands flew to her lips. Her cheeks were red, but he watched the color fade within moments.

"Oh! You're not—"

She seemed to think better of revealing who she'd planned to meet and snapped her lips closed.

"I take it you were expecting someone else?"

He thought she'd shake her head in denial. Perhaps babble some excuse and then flee. Instead, she folded her arms at her waist and frowned at him. The position framed her bodice, and he was powerless to stop his gaze from lowering to her breasts. Her bounty was more modest than the widow, but he found himself wondering how it would feel to drag this woman into his arms and make love to her.

"Are you quite done?"

He laughed. "You can cease playing the scandalized maiden, Miss Rowland. We both know why you are out here in the gardens late at night."

Her mouth dropped open, and then she glared at him. Actually glared. It was an amusing change of pace. Normally, women went out of their way to make themselves attractive—and available—to him. And young women newly out in society, well, they avoided him altogether.

But it seemed that Miss Rowland was made of sterner stuff. To his absolute shock, he was intrigued.

"You might be out here for other… nefarious reasons. But I just wanted to enjoy the gardens."

He crossed his arms, mimicking her stance, and held her gaze for several seconds. She looked away first.

She'd been angry that he'd dragged her against him, so perhaps she was telling the truth and thought that a man would meet her here late at night, alone, and not want to touch her.

"Who did you think I was when you spun around?"

Her lips firmed into a tight line, and he wanted to shake her. Surely her family didn't know she was sneaking out into the gardens to take in the flowers with some bloke who would think nothing of ruining her.

"You need to stay away from the gardens at night. They're frequented by rogues and ne'er-do-wells."

She lifted her chin, which somehow, despite the fact that he was at least a foot taller than her, had the effect of making it appear as though she were looking down at him. "Perhaps that was what I was seeking? Someone who wasn't tame."

He was fairly certain her demeanor was a show of bravado. Clearly Miss Rowland needed someone to shake her out of her complacency. To show her that the world wasn't a safe place for gently bred young women.

He moved closer, aware of the way she drew him to her like a magnet. Normally he'd be putting as much space as possible between himself and someone who was fresh on the marriage mart.

"Are you looking for danger, Miss Rowland?"

Her eyes widened in surprise. "You know who I am?"

He held her gaze. "I make it a point to learn the identities of beautiful young women."

Her head tilted to one side as she examined

him. "I can't decide whether that's a genuine compliment or just something you say to all women."

He shrugged. "There are enough beautiful women in London that I don't need to lie to the ones who aren't."

She winced. "It's lowering to know that I'm just one of many."

He needed to step away from her. Instead, he moved closer and cupped her chin loosely. A surprising zing of attraction zipped up his arm. He couldn't remember the last time he'd been this intrigued by a woman.

"There is nothing ordinary about you."

Heat flooded her cheeks again. "Thank you."

He dropped his hand, but he didn't step away. He couldn't. "Who were you expecting, Iris?"

"Perhaps I was hoping that the infamous Lord Wentworth would see me slip away and follow me out here?"

He laughed, charmed despite himself by her bravado. "You're playing a dangerous game. What if I told you that was exactly what had happened? That I'd followed you out here, and now I want nothing more than to kiss you senseless."

She shied away then and took a step back. "Mr.

Tobias Miller has been courting me. He told me that he wanted us to spend a few minutes alone together. I thought that perhaps he wanted to take our courtship further."

A haze of unexpected anger settled over him. He knew exactly what Miller wanted from Iris, and it wasn't to propose marriage. He kept his gaze focused on her, knowing that his next words would reveal the real reason behind Iris's foray into these gardens.

"I was at White's this morning. Miller was bragging about how he'd just offered for Miss Bennington and that his suit had been accepted."

All color drained from Iris's face. "I didn't know." She looked away, no doubt coming to the realization that Miller's proposal had not been the innocent one she'd expected.

"Do you care for him?" He had the irrational urge to find Miller and punch him.

She sighed, and he felt his heart constrict. He ignored the feeling. He didn't have a heart.

"No, which was why I decided to meet him here. I was going to tell him that it was probably best if he ceased his courtship." Her lips twisted in a wry grimace. "I thought that I was allowing myself to be unreasonable in my expectations, but there was something about him that set my teeth on edge. He seemed a little *too* solicitous."

Her response shouldn't have brought about the surge of relief flowing through him. "He's a bounder of the worst sort. A young woman like yourself doesn't expect to be led astray and taken advantage of."

"I was foolish coming out here. You're correct. I should go."

She started to move past him, but he'd caught the way her body shrank with shame. Anger surged through him that anyone would try to make this woman feel worthless. "I can call him out."

She froze, shocked at his statement. His outburst had surprised him as well.

She turned to face him and shook her head, those careful blond curls dancing about her face. He wondered what her hair would look like when she took it down that night before sliding under her covers. Would she let the mass tumble across the bedsheets, or would she carefully plait the strands to avoid tangles?

After staring at him for several seconds, she shook her head. "I don't know you. What would people say when word got out? People always whisper. Our names would be linked, and everyone would wonder…" She took a deep breath, and he was impressed by the way she took control over her obvious panic. "Thank you for the offer, my lord, but I think it best if I just return to the ballroom now."

He inclined his head. "Perhaps that would be best."

She gave him a tremulous smile. "I am in your debt, my lord."

Why did he want to take this young woman into his arms and tell her that he would protect her? She had protectors already. She knew that Seaford would kill any man who tried to take advantage of his wife's sister. He'd issued the warning himself at White's at the beginning of the season. But apparently Miller had a death wish.

Pushing aside the uncomfortable urge to protect Iris, he inclined his head. "Any true gentleman would do the same."

She sighed. "And now I must face him. He's going to approach me at some point this evening and ask me why I changed my mind about meeting him here."

"If he comes anywhere near you, simply smile and offer him felicitations on his betrothal."

That elicited a ghost of a smile. "I like the

sound of that. And then I'll make sure to spread the word about his upcoming marriage so he can't lure some other simpleton out into the gardens."

She was beginning to turn away again, but he couldn't let her leave this way.

"Iris."

She halted and turned back to face him. "Miller is a fool. You are worth ten, nay hundreds, of the other young women here. She has a great fortune to her name but little else to recommend her. You are beautiful and strong. Don't forget that."

She gave him a soft smile. "Never worry about that. When I'm finished spreading the word about how I overheard him trying to lure an unsuspecting victim for his debauchery into the gardens after he'd already offered for another…" She lifted one shoulder. "You are correct of course. I'm not the one who should be ashamed. Thank you for pointing that out."

"I am very happy to be of service."

And he was. He watched her go—and just in time. The widow entered the garden bower then, mere seconds after Iris had left. He winced as he thought about how the two would have crossed paths.

She threw herself into his arms, but his

thoughts were too full of the young woman he'd just saved from ruin. His mood had soured. And if he was being honest with himself, he'd much rather speak to Iris Rowland than lift the skirts of this woman whose name he didn't even know.

He pushed her away. "I'm afraid something has come up. I'm only here to tell you that we can't slip away together."

She pouted at him. "I've already said my good-byes. If you need to leave, perhaps you can join me in my carriage."

He watched how she leaned forward a little, giving him a tantalizing view of her breasts that were threatening to spill over the top of her dress. But the sight did little to entice him.

He needed to speak to Miller. Warn him away from Iris… from debauching any maiden, really, with false promises of a future he would never give them. That was the only reason he was no longer in the mood to dally. After he settled things with Miller —really, there were many experienced women who were more than willing to slip away for a quick tumble—then he could put thoughts of Iris behind him.

The widow finally slunk away, annoyance clear

in her sullen expression and in the way she straightened her shoulders as she turned to leave.

He moved into the shadows and waited for Miller to arrive. Hopefully Iris wouldn't run into him first. He very much wanted to have a *talk* with the man.

CHAPTER 2

*W*entworth was jolted back to the present when the carriage slowed to a halt. He'd gone over that scene far too often in the past six months, allowing that brief encounter with Iris Rowland to take up too much of his thoughts.

That would change today. He would come to his senses when he saw her again and realized she was far too young and inexperienced for him. That he'd allowed some hitherto unknown sense of sentimentality to take hold.

He'd be on his way back to London tomorrow morning and would resume his normal life, unfettered by concerns for the young woman he'd saved from certain ruin.

A footman opened the carriage door, allowing cold air into the warm interior of the carriage. He stepped down, making a mental note to see that the driver was rewarded handsomely.

He glanced up at the clouds above as he crossed the short distance to the front door and couldn't help but wonder if they were a sign snow was on the way. He pushed aside the grim thought of being trapped here for days and kept moving forward.

The butler swung the door open before he could raise a hand, and he was greeted by a small welcoming party. The dowager viscountess and Lady Thornton smiled in greeting and curtsied. Behind the two women, standing like vigilant sentries, were the two obstacles he'd have to overcome. Viscount Thornton and the Earl of Seaford.

Satisfaction swept through him at Seaford's presence. If he was there, then it was likely his sister-in-law, Iris, would be also.

Lady Thornton was the first to speak. "We are so happy to have you here. But I must admit it came as something of a surprise to see your name on the guest list. It was my understanding that you didn't like house parties."

It seemed that Thornton's wife had a backbone. Wentworth could respect that.

He bowed over her hand and smiled, doing his best to call forth all the charm for which he was famous. "I've heard so many wonderful things about your yearly Christmas gathering and sought an invitation. I am so pleased you were able to accommodate me."

Lady Thornton nodded in reply, but he could tell she was doubtful about his presence. Her mother-in-law, however, was beaming.

The dowager offered her hand, and he bowed over it as well. "Thank you for interceding on my behalf."

She gave him an arch look that spoke volumes. She'd issued the invitation, yes, but she was curious about his presence. It appeared his excuse hadn't fooled anyone. "If you'd like to get settled, I can have a footman show you to your room."

And that's when the two men stepped forward and Thornton spoke. "If you don't mind, we'd like to speak with you privately first."

Thornton shared a significant look with his wife, and Wentworth knew what was coming. The viscount was going to warn him about proper behavior.

He shot an amused glance at Seaford. Before last year, when the man had courted Miss Lily

Rowland, Seaford's reputation had been as wild as his own. It seemed a little hypocritical for Seaford to be a part of this conversation.

But Wentworth refused to let their presence deter him. After all, he would only be here for one day at most.

WENTWORTH WASN'T SURPRISED WHEN THE TWO MEN led him to Thornton's study and closed the door.

"I must say, I'm honored to be singled out for such an auspicious welcome. Or is this your customary greeting?"

Seaford's lips twitched, but then he gained control of his features. Thornton's expression of course turned even grimmer. It appeared that marriage had cost the man his sense of humor.

Thornton folded his arms across his chest. "Why are you here?"

Wentworth raised a brow. "I received a gracious invitation from your mother, the dowager viscountess."

Thornton made a scoffing sound. "You went out of your way to obtain that invitation. For the life of me, I don't know why she agreed to have you here."

He shrugged. There was no point denying it. He'd had to call in several favors.

"Who are you pursuing?" Seaford was leaning against the desk, his body more at ease. He wasn't scowling like Thornton, but Wentworth suspected that would change once he learned the truth.

"Come on, man," Thornton said. "We all know you didn't accept an invitation to a country house party because you were feeling lonely and wanted to celebrate the festive season with us."

It seemed Thornton was going to be a thorn in his side. His lips quirked at the pun, but he thought it best not to laugh aloud.

He glanced at Seaford again. The earl had once been considered a rake, so he knew he didn't have any prudish sensibilities. But after marrying Iris's sister last Christmas, he seemed to have settled down.

He realized that the same could be said of him after he'd met Iris. He hadn't had one lover in that time, which was an intolerable situation. His mind shied away from thoughts that he might be ready to settle down himself.

But there was something about Iris that had intrigued him.

"I find it interesting that you had no problem welcoming Seaford into your extended family and into your home. Did he get the same inquisition about his intentions?"

Seaford barked out a laugh. "The ass actually warned Lily's family about me. Told them I couldn't be trusted."

Thornton shrugged. "It was the truth."

"And yet here you are, joining Thornton in questioning me about my motives."

Seaford aimed a scowl at the viscount. "Yes. Despite Thornton's sabotage, I managed to prevail."

Thornton merely shrugged. "He was sniffing around after my wife's cousin."

"I can understand your caution, but it's unwarranted. Have you ever heard anyone accuse me of taking advantage of a woman?"

Seaford shook his head. "If you have nothing to hide, then you can tell us why you're here."

Wentworth let out a loud breath as he gave up all pretense. Everyone was going to realize why he was here the moment he spoke to Iris. He met

Seaford's gaze and braced for whatever might come. "Your wife's middle sister."

Seaford actually paled. "Iris? Devil take it, Lily is going to kill me if we don't turn you out right now."

Wentworth raised one shoulder. "I wouldn't worry too much about it. I don't expect I'll be here long."

Seaford's entire demeanor changed. He rose to his feet and took a menacing step closer. "If you're thinking about defiling her and leaving, I'm going to have to call you out right now."

Wentworth held up his hands. "No, stop. That came out all wrong. But the damned woman has been in my thoughts since the season ended, and I need to exorcise her." He shook his head, hating that he had to explain himself to these two men, but he couldn't be turned out before seeing this thing through. "I'm sure a conversation or two will be enough to show me she's just another silly and frivolous young woman. I just caught her in a serious moment. After speaking to her again, I'll be able to set aside my curiosity about her."

Thornton actually laughed. "Clearly you don't know Iris if that's what you think."

Seaford shook his head. "Iris might be young,

but she has a level head on her shoulders. All the Rowland women do. It's unsettling."

Wentworth frowned, pushing back the doubt that was beginning to creep in. He'd already started on this course of action and must continue. "Duly noted. Am I allowed to leave this room now?"

Thornton let out a resigned sigh. "Just know that we're watching you."

Wentworth inclined his head, accepting the inevitable scrutiny. He would expect nothing less and would deal with their overprotective behavior for his short stay.

CHAPTER 3

$\mathcal{I}$ris left her bedchamber and made her way downstairs.

She was always late getting started whenever she had to travel. The trip to her cousin Celia's home wasn't a long one, so the carriage ride hadn't been overly strenuous. But she hadn't been able to sleep last night because of her excitement.

She wandered down to the drawing room, where she could hear voices floating out into the hall. She hesitated a moment outside, listening to the excited murmurs. She caught giggles and only snippets of whispers. *Can't believe he's here… He never attends house parties… Do you think he's planning on settling down…*

The speculation sparked her curiosity. Hoping to find someone she knew, she stepped into the room.

The space was filled with many of the female guests who were clustered together on the settee or standing in groups. They all seemed to be talking about this mysterious guest.

Iris's curiosity was engaged. Her thoughts immediately flew to the man she'd met near the end of the season in London. Lord Wentworth. His arrival at such an event would surely spark this level of speculation among all the women, both young and old. But Wentworth would never attend a Christmas house party in the country.

From everything she'd heard about the man, he was a confirmed rakehell. And the way he'd gone from complimenting her to heading off with a buxom woman into the bowels of the garden, a wicked smirk on her face, had set her blood boiling.

No, he would never attend such an event, which was exactly to her liking because she never wanted to see him again.

Her eyes swept over the room and settled on the two women she wanted to see, who were clustered by the window. Her sister Lily and her cousin Celia.

They met her gaze, and she smiled in greeting, but before she took even one step in their direction, the air in the room changed abruptly. Whispers were silenced, and everyone turned to look at her.

She took in their wide eyes and gaping expressions. A few quickly covered their surprise, while others continued to stare at her avidly as though they'd never seen her before.

She looked down at her dress, wondering if something was amiss, but could see nothing wrong. Then she lifted a hand to her hair. She'd pinned it up carefully after waking from her nap. Had it come loose?

"I think they're staring at me. You, as always, are impeccable and lovely."

She froze, shock washing over her at the voice coming from over her left shoulder. No, she was imagining things.

Slowly, half expecting to discover that she was still in bed and was, in fact, dreaming, she shifted to the left and met Lord Wentworth's amused expression.

"I'm dreaming." Her voice was barely above a whisper. Would she even remember this when she woke up? She rarely remembered her dreams. How often had Wentworth invaded her thoughts while she was sleeping?

One corner of his mouth quirked up into that smirk that had so unsettled her when they met.

"I can't fault you for thinking so, but I am very real."

She was about to reach out and pinch him but in the end decided it would be best to pinch her own arm. With all the eyes on them now, it wouldn't do to be caught touching the man in the unlikely event this was actually happening.

She squeezed her fingers together over the skin of her forearm and twisted, then winced at the spark of pain.

His eyes narrowed on the movement, his forehead now creased in a frown. For one absurd moment, she thought he was going to reach out to soothe the small hurt she'd given herself.

"My lord, how nice of you to join us," Celia said, appearing on her right.

Her sister Lily appeared on her left. "If you're looking for the gentlemen, I believe they're in the billiard room."

His forehead cleared, and his expression took on his customary amusement. As though there was a running dialogue inside his head and he was constantly coming up with funny witticisms to explain what was happening around him. She wondered what that voice was saying about this current turn of events.

No. She couldn't allow herself to wonder anything about this man. He was an experienced man of the world. A rake. He wasn't interested in her at all, not when he spent his free time gambling with his peers and bedding loose women.

Her stomach soured at the thought of the other women he'd been with, but she refused to allow him to see it. He met her gaze, and she got the impression that he wanted to speak to *her*. In private.

"Of course," he said. "I didn't realize that we were segregating our activities based on sex." The way he emphasized that last word, as though he were intentionally trying to shock them, had her interest sparking anew. Damn this man. Why was he so captivating?

Celia and Lily shifted closer to her, and she realized they were trying to protect her. She wanted to laugh at them. Lord Wentworth was most definitely *not* interested in her, much to her chagrin.

The dowager viscountess swept into the room then, and the expression on her face was almost comical. It was inconceivable to her that he would have stumbled into the drawing room when it was clearly set aside for just the women right then. Clearly she knew nothing about the man's reputation. Iris had only met the man once, but she would have guessed that if one were in search of Wentworth, they should look to where the women were congregating.

Or secreted away in one of the bedchambers with someone. Somehow she kept her mouth from twisting at that thought.

They moved to the side as Celia's mother-in-law placed herself squarely before him, for all intents and purposes as though she were guarding the entrance.

"My lord, I understand that this is your first house party. There will be ample opportunity for everyone to gather together later. But we've learned over the years that men like their time alone together."

Wentworth met her gaze again over the dowager's shoulder, and she came to a bizarre realization that she could read his thoughts. And Wentworth wanted her to know that what the dowager viscountess was saying was that it was the women who wanted some time away from the men so that they could gossip.

And since they'd been doing just that when she arrived, she couldn't deny it. She lifted one shoulder in a small shrug, and his eyes sparked with amusement.

He turned back to Lady Thornton. "Of course. I must have gotten the hours wrong. I thought we were to all meet here."

"Oh no, there is a set time when the men can gather together in various areas of the house. I'll make sure that someone gives the schedule to your valet. Until then…"

Iris wanted to stay and hear what he was going to say next. Or barring that, stay and see if she could read his thoughts again the next time he looked at her. But while the dowager viscountess droned on about the schedule, Celia and Lily linked their arms through hers and took her back to the spot they'd commandeered near the window.

It took every ounce of strength she had not to glance back to see what was happening in the doorway. "Is Violet still in her room? And I don't see Clara."

Lily gave her head a small shake. "Violet wanted to write a letter to a friend. Honestly, she's always writing letters of late. I'm a little worried about her. Will she even know how to engage with people next season when she comes out? At least Seaford's sister is often with her, so she isn't completely feral."

Iris laughed. "I know you're not able to visit as often now that you're married, but I can assure you that our sister doesn't spend all her time writing letters." She waited until Lily let out a small sigh of relief before adding, "At least not when she's visiting with Clara. Otherwise, she spends the rest of her time reading."

Lily grimaced, and Iris couldn't hold back her laugh. Violet had always enjoyed reading and scribbling in her journal. To be honest, Iris had been relieved when their youngest sister had started writing letters to various acquaintances.

Celia leaned in close, her voice barely above a whisper. "You need to take care, Iris. My husband told me that Lord Wentworth has accepted this invitation because of you."

Iris couldn't help it, she burst out laughing at the earnest expression on her cousin's face.

"This is quite serious. You need to be careful and make sure you're never alone with him."

"Well, perhaps that's going a bit too far," Lily added. "I'm sure a minute here or there throughout the next few days won't cause a scandal. Everyone else will be doing it. Besides, if he's decided to court my sister, we need to give him the opportunity to do so."

Iris looked from her sister, who seemed to believe what she was saying, to Celia, whose mouth had set into a disapproving line. Surely they didn't believe the fiction they were telling her.

"I think Thornton is having fun at your expense," she said, trying to ease her cousin's very obvious distress. "Lord Wentworth is someone who enjoys spending time with experienced women. There is nothing you can say to make me believe that he came here to see *me*." She let out another laugh, but this one had an edge to it she didn't want to think about. Disappointment, perhaps?

"I think Celia is correct. Simon told me the same thing, and he wanted me to keep an eye on you."

She pierced her sister with a penetrating glance and was careful to keep her voice low when she replied to that ridiculous admonishment. "Would this be the same husband who kidnapped you and spent the night with you, *alone*, in a small cottage before you were married?"

Lily's eyes widened, and she glanced about them to see if anyone had overheard. When she was satisfied no one was near, she hissed back at her, "Are you trying to cause a scandal?"

"No, I'm just trying to point out that you married a rake, and he changed his ways. It's possible that Lord Wentworth might be trying to do the same."

"Simon courted me for months, and he was a perfect gentleman during that period. He only…" She waved her hand, unwilling to repeat Iris's words lest they be overheard. "I'd turned down his proposal of marriage because I thought he only wanted me because I would make a convenient bride."

"Yes, yes, but instead, he's wildly passionate about you." Honestly, was it necessary for her sister to rub in the fact that she'd found happiness when Iris's own season had ended in disappointment?

Celia covered her mouth to hide her snort of laughter.

Lily rolled her eyes. "You don't have room to criticize me. Thornton is equally devoted to you."

The two smiled at one another, and Iris rolled her eyes. "I'm going to go check on Violet and try to coax her to join us. The two of you can continue to congratulate yourselves on having secured love matches while I'm gone."

She began to turn, but Lily stopped her and whispered into her ear, "Promise me you'll act with caution."

"Of course," Iris said with a nod. It was an easy promise to make since she knew she was in no danger from Wentworth.

CHAPTER 4

The afternoon had passed by pleasantly enough, filled mainly with several rounds of billiards and various card games. They'd played only for bragging rights, something he hadn't done since he was a youth. But it seemed that it was equally enjoyable to win even if there wasn't money involved... and he'd won far more than he'd lost.

It got tiring after a while having to play off the curious glances and outright questions from everyone about why he was there. If these people could accept a rake like Seaford into their midst, then he couldn't understand why they were so surprised that he'd be in attendance.

It was an effort not to dwell on his all-too-brief

interaction with Iris Rowland several hours earlier. A sense of unease had settled over him after being unceremoniously led away from the drawing room by Thornton's mother.

She'd said all the right things, of course, but it was clear that something had changed with respect to how she viewed him. He'd had to call in several favors among friends of the family to get this invitation, but the woman's welcome when he first arrived was a far cry from her demeanor when she'd come across him performing the unspeakable act of trying to enter the drawing room.

Iris had been right there, but it was now clear that the world was conspiring against him.

He rolled his shoulders as he waited for Iris to leave her bedchamber. His valet had learned where Iris was sleeping, but he wasn't such a brute as to storm into her room. Instead, he'd found a discrete alcove to lurk in near the end of the hallway and lay in wait, very much like a villain in a horrid novel.

It was humbling to be the one doing the chasing. Not that he was chasing after Iris, of course. He just needed to speak to her so he could finally set aside the curiosity that had him obsessing about their meeting in the garden months ago.

He wasn't quite sure how he would accomplish

that during the evening's entertainments. The sanctioned mingling period between the sexes before dinner.

Fortunately, the wait wasn't a long one, so he wouldn't have to try to convince someone that he'd lost his way. The manor house was large, yes, but it was laid out in much the same manner as countless other houses he'd visited.

Iris exited her bedroom, and he was just about to approach her when she was followed by her younger sister as well as Seaford's sister.

He let out an amused huff at his own presumption that this would be easy. Nothing thus far had been. This was yet another roadblock he'd have to overcome.

They would have to pass by him before heading downstairs, so he waited for her to approach. He watched her smile at something her sister said. Then, sensing his presence, she turned her head toward him, her smile freezing in place.

She said something to her two companions and then headed toward him. The younger women waited, clearly curious about what was happening.

Iris stopped when she reached him and shook her head. Her expression was very much one of bemusement, as though she'd found him sneaking a treat before dinner.

"Why am I not surprised to find you lurking outside the bedrooms assigned to the female guests?"

He chuckled. "I see you haven't lost your wit."

She raised one shoulder. "If a man is scared away by a woman's intelligence, then he isn't worth knowing."

She folded her arms across her chest and waited for his response. He could tell that she was assessing his reaction to her statement. There was a resignation within that told him he'd already been judged and found wanting.

"I'm not afraid of a woman's intelligence."

She searched his face, no doubt looking for any clue that would tell her he was lying. He knew she'd find none. Others might prefer a woman who was simply a decorative accessory, but he liked his women with a little more substance.

"There are few men who would agree with you."

"That would be their failing."

They stared at one another for several seconds. Finally, she let out a soft huff of air.

"I don't know who is assigned to which room, so

it seems you'll have to wait a little longer to meet your paramour."

He knew she meant the words as a set down, but to him it felt like a challenge. If she thought he would be so easily dismissed, then he'd have to show her otherwise.

"There is no paramour in residence here, but" —he took a step closer and lowered his voice—"if you'd like to apply for the position, I'd be willing to consider your application."

Her eyes widened a fraction, and he waited for her reaction. He should have known that she'd surprise him yet again when she let out a hearty laugh. He couldn't help but join her, so infectious was her mirth.

Finally, her amusement faded, but her eyes were still twinkling. And she was actually smiling at him. "You are incorrigible. I can see why everyone has rushed to warn me about you."

He wasn't surprised at the knowledge. But at least her family hadn't seen fit to position a footman outside her bedroom door. Thank goodness for small mercies.

He smiled down at her. "But you're not afraid of me." It wasn't a question since it was clear Iris wasn't afraid for her virtue. Not at the moment.

She shook her head. "You had me alone in a dark garden. If you wanted to ravish me, you would have done it then."

She turned away and started back down the hallway. He fell into step beside her.

She glanced sideways at him. "Won't your paramour be disappointed if you abandon your wait so soon? I promise not to tell anyone."

He leaned closer and murmured, "I'm here for you, Iris Rowland."

Her steps faltered, but then she straightened and continued to her two companions.

"Allow me to introduce you, my lord, to my sister, Miss Violet Rowland, and to my good friend, Miss Clara Howe. This is Lord Wentworth."

He bowed his greeting to the two younger women. "It is a pleasure to meet the two of you."

Iris fell into step next to her two companions, and he trailed just behind them.

She glanced at him over her shoulders, and he could see her surprise that he was still with them. He grinned at her. She'd learn soon enough that he was only here for her.

Her lips tightened into a line before she turned away. She did lean slightly toward the other two and say, her voice clear, "He's something of a reprobate, so watch yourselves around him."

He let out a startled laugh. He'd been dreading this visit, thinking that he'd need to put it behind him quickly so that he could continue with his normal life, but after one short conversation with Iris, everything had changed. He'd have to inform his valet that they wouldn't be leaving tomorrow morning.

CHAPTER 5

*I*ris found it impossible to ignore Wentworth's presence. After their chance meeting that evening all those months ago, she'd never expected to speak to him again. Given the type of woman with whom he normally associated, she certainly never expected him to seek her out.

Which was why her gaze kept drifting over to him when he wasn't close by. She expected that a more sophisticated woman wouldn't be quite so obvious, but Iris wasn't up to that level of pretense. Wentworth had told her that he was here for her, but she couldn't allow herself to believe him.

She took note of who he was speaking to and expected him to slip away at some point. When that didn't happen before dinner, she told herself that he was being discreet for now and would slip away to meet someone after dinner when people had wandered off to experience one of the entertainments during the evening.

She hadn't expected him to be seated next to her during the meal and suspected that he must have switched out the name cards to achieve that outcome.

She concentrated on speaking to the older gentleman to her right and his wife, who was seated across from them. And she absolutely was not straining to hear what Wentworth was saying to the widow who was to his left. But every time he chuckled, the soft sound had her hackles rising.

Finally, during a lull in the conversation near the end of the main course, he leaned close to her.

"You've been uncharacteristically silent toward me. And after all the trouble I undertook to ensure we were seated next to one another."

Her eyes narrowed on him, and she couldn't help but wonder what game he was playing. Perhaps he was trying to make the widow jealous. For one moment she considered telling him not to bother trying to charm her, but she'd be lying to both of them. Even if he was using her as a pawn in another game, there was no reason she couldn't enjoy herself.

She lowered her voice and prayed no one could overhear their conversation. "If you need my assistance in trying to make someone else jealous, I'm willing to play along." Then she laughed softly and spoke in what she hoped was a normal tone. She'd never tried her hand at acting a role before today. "Pray continue. I'd love to hear the rest of that story."

He chuckled in reply, for all the world seeming as though she'd genuinely amused him. It was clear he was far more skilled at pretense than she.

"I'll win you over yet, Miss Rowland."

He'd tire of this game soon enough, but for now she was willing to accept his attention. It wasn't as though anyone else was trying to capture her interest. Wentworth was the only single gentleman under the age of fifty in attendance.

Now that Iris wasn't intent on ignoring the man while simultaneously trying to overhear what he was saying to his other dinner companion, the rest of the meal passed far more pleasantly. She was included in his conversation with the widow, and the situation baffled her. It seemed that the woman was already engaged to another. Iris looked for clues to any hidden meaning behind their words but she couldn't detect a hint of romance between the two.

After the meal was over, the men remained in the dining room to enjoy their port and to smoke. She imagined that she could feel Wentworth's eyes on her as she left with the rest of the women. She couldn't resist turning back to look at him when she was in the doorway and was shocked to discover it hadn't been her imagination.

The men were all standing, of course, but he was the only one who hadn't already turned to engage in conversation with another. His head tilted to one side, and she could tell he'd been waiting for her to look back at him.

She shrugged in reply. She was a novice at whatever game he was playing, so of course he would have the upper hand.

When they reached the ballroom, which had been turned into a salon for the house party, she was surrounded yet again by her older sister and her cousin. They drew her a little way down the hall and waited for the other women to enter the ball-room before turning to face her.

Celia's brows were drawn together. "I was very careful with the seating plan to ensure that you weren't seated next to Lord Wentworth."

A small zing went through her at that piece of information. He hadn't been lying about that after all. She'd wanted to believe him but wasn't sure it was prudent to take anything he said at face value.

Lily didn't bother to hide her amusement. "Clearly he had someone switch the place cards."

Iris smiled. "Is that why you had them this year? Thornton's mother usually allowed people to sit where they wanted when she was hosting the parties."

Celia let out a soft sigh. "They were a last-minute addition. I was trying to avoid this very thing, but it appears I shouldn't have bothered."

Lily bumped shoulders with Celia. "I'm sure it will be fine. There was no harm done."

"Says the woman who married a reformed rake." Celia turned to Iris. "You might not be so fortunate, Iris. I don't know why he seems to be fixated on you, but you should be careful."

Her cousin's warning had the exact opposite effect on her. Iris would need to be careful lest she betray the fact that she was actually enjoying the man's attention.

She tried to keep her tone light lest she betray that fact. "He seems well-liked, even among the men. Surely he isn't such a blackguard."

"That's the way of it with men," Lily said. "I've seen it often enough with my own husband. Every man wants to be their friend, and every woman wants to bed them."

Iris stared at her sister in shock. "Still? Even though he's clearly devoted to you?" A horrible thought occurred to her. "Surely he doesn't *entertain* these other women."

"Oh no," Lily said. "I have no fears in that department. But it can be unsettling watching another woman try to lure him from my side. Many aren't even subtle about it."

Celia let out a soft laugh. "But it's very amusing to watch their annoyance when our husbands turn them away."

"So how can you be sure that a man's interest is genuine?"

Celia and Lily shared a look before her cousin spoke. "You can't, not really. You just have to listen to your heart *and* your head. Many a young woman has allowed herself to be carried away by thoughts of fairy-tale endings. But they ignore the warning signs."

Iris nodded, taking in the wisdom of those words even while she longed to give in to the romance of having a charismatic man pursue her.

"So I need to watch how he behaves with the other women." She turned to Celia. "Was everyone present at dinner?"

"Yes. Why do you ask?"

"I was just wondering if perhaps his paramour was here. But since he was sitting next to me, she might not have come down for dinner."

Celia shook her head. "Everyone was here. Perhaps that's why he's fixed his attention on you. He might see you as a likely target, someone who is easy to manipulate."

Iris wanted to leap to Wentworth's defense, but she couldn't allow her cousin to know that she was thinking about entertaining his pursuit to see where it ended.

Instead, she shared the small piece of information she'd been keeping to herself. "We met in London. Near the end of the season."

Lily's hand flew to her mouth, and Celia became unnaturally still. It was hard not to squirm under their twin stares.

Her sister reached for her hand. "You didn't tell me. Did he… Surely he didn't proposition you?" The words were said in a harsh whisper.

She really didn't want to share her foolish misstep, but she had to let Celia and Lily know that Wentworth wasn't a complete blackguard. "No, he was a gentleman. But he did find me alone."

Lily's eyes narrowed. "When did this happen?"

"During a ball. I slipped out into the gardens to meet someone."

Celia clutched her arm. "Wentworth?"

She shook her head. "Someone else. It doesn't matter who. Wentworth saw me, we spoke for a little while, and he convinced me to return inside. Apparently the person I was going to meet had just offered for someone else, so his intentions weren't honorable."

Celia let out a breath. "So Wentworth didn't take advantage of you. And it sounds like he might have stopped someone else from doing just that."

Lily nudged her again. "I told you. Not all rakes are out to ruin the innocence of every young maiden they happen upon."

"Perhaps not. But he's here now, and he's made his interest in you clear."

Iris lifted one shoulder, feigning a nonchalance she was far from feeling. "He's just passing the time."

"He wasn't on the original guest list. Thornton's mother added him at the last minute, and she didn't tell me or her son until after the invitation had gone out."

Lily's eyes were gleaming with interest now. "Why would she do that?"

Her cousin's eyes remained fixed on Iris. "She was approached by someone and asked to invite him. She wouldn't say who that person was, but apparently Wentworth was very eager to be here."

Iris's heart was starting to race. "He was speaking to another female guest during the meal."

Celia shook her head. "No, this person asked whether the Rowland sisters would be in attendance. After my mother-in-law told them that you'd all been invited, they told her that Lord Wentworth would consider himself beholden to the family if he received an invitation."

Lily's eyes were wide now with the same excitement Iris was trying to tamp down within herself. "Do you think he wants to court you?"

Iris wanted to believe that. But despite everything she'd heard today, both now and from Wentworth himself, she still needed to guard her heart. She kept replaying the way that meeting in the garden had ended, with the man admonishing her to go back inside.

But she'd hurried past another woman who was

walking down that darkened garden path. Someone older and more worldly. Iris had watched from the shadows as that woman threw herself into Wentworth's arms before she'd turned and fled. She hadn't wanted to see what the two of them would do next.

No, she couldn't compete with the type of women that normally interested this man. She couldn't allow herself to fall into the romantic notion that she would be able to reform a rake, the way Lily had.

She would try to enjoy herself during this house party, and if that meant witty conversations with Wentworth, she'd throw herself wholeheartedly into the pastime. But she needed to be careful to guard her heart in the process.

Finally, the men finished their drinks, and they made their way to the ballroom to join the women. Wentworth had no qualms about disappointing the few older gentlemen who wanted to return to the billiard room for the rest of the evening. He was there for only one person. Iris.

The ballroom had been turned into a salon for the house party. Small seating arrangements were scattered throughout the space, and there were card tables set up for those who wanted to play whist. Evergreen boughs and festive decorations were hung on the walls and scattered throughout the room. Off to one side, there was a long table laden with refreshments, and someone was playing soft music on a pianoforte.

The effect was warm and charming, but his gaze settled immediately on Iris. She was sitting on a settee on the far side of the room, flanked by both her older sister and cousin. Seaford's wife nudged Iris's shoulder and whispered something in her ear.

For a moment he feared she was telling Iris that she wouldn't be leaving her side. Relief filled him several seconds later when the countess rose to greet her husband. Lady Thornton also rose to greet her own husband. Which left Iris unguarded.

Or at least as much as one could be in a room filled with far too many people.

Iris smiled at him then, which was all the encouragement he needed. Never one to miss an opportunity, he crossed the room and settled next to her.

"I wonder how long we'll be able to speak together before someone comes to whisk you away."

Iris tilted her head to one side, her blue eyes crinkling with amusement. "I think it far more likely that you'll grow bored with me and seek out another."

"And how would that make you feel?"

His eyes remained fixed on hers as she considered the question. Another woman would be coy, making an exaggerated comment about how all her hopes and dreams would be dashed. Or they'd pretend indifference. Of course Iris would be different.

"Honestly? I'm not sure how I would feel."

"I would hope you'd be disappointed. I know I would be."

She examined him, and he waited, hoping she'd be able to tell he spoke the truth.

Finally, she nodded. "I don't understand why you're here." She lowered her voice before continuing. "I've been told that you sought this invitation because you wanted to see me again."

"I did."

Had he ever felt this vulnerable with a woman? Not since his first experience bedding an older widow who was very eager to mold him into the perfect lover. But back then he'd been concerned about his lack of experience hampering his performance. Right now he was worried about this woman, who was barely out of the schoolroom, finding him wanting as a person. And for the life of him, he couldn't understand why.

She nodded, accepting his admission. "Why?"

When he'd set out to secure an invitation to the

annual Thornton Christmas house party, he hadn't expected to be on the receiving end of Iris's questions.

"Honestly? I don't know why. But I've been thinking about that meeting, and I needed to see you again."

She let out a soft sigh and glanced away. "Of course. You wanted to make sure that I hadn't continued with my foolish quest to find love with unworthy men who just wanted to take advantage of me."

His chest constricted as he remembered how close that had come to happening. He wanted to reach for her but couldn't, not with so many people surrounding them. But blessedly, they'd been provided with a measure of solitude for now.

It seemed they were being aided by Thornton and Seaford and their wives. They were standing nearby, chatting together. Close enough that he and Iris weren't truly alone, but they did waylay anyone who was heading in their direction by engaging them in conversation or mentioning how good the wassail was this year.

"Iris." He waited until she turned to meet his gaze. "I will forever be grateful that I found you out in the garden that evening. But I am not here as someone who is checking on your well-being."

She licked her lips, and he wanted to groan. "Then why are you here?"

He'd come this far, but instead of being convinced his interest in this young woman was nothing but a foolish whim, he was beginning to think it went deeper. "I'm here because I can't stop thinking about you."

She shook her head but said nothing.

She didn't believe him. He wanted to laugh aloud at the absurd thought. Of course she didn't. She had to have known that he was out in that garden because he too was planning to meet someone. She might not have known his reputation then, but she would have been enlightened about his character once he made his interest in her known to Thornton and Seaford.

And dammit, he admired her for it. Because now he knew that she wasn't a silly creature given to flights of fancy. She wouldn't just take his word for it that something deeper had happened between them out in that garden.

That he was here because he'd become obsessed with her. He who'd never been captivated by another woman couldn't stop thinking about this one. And coming here to speak with her again had only cemented his interest.

Violet Rowland dropped onto the settee next to her sister, ending their brief moment of privacy. She twined her arm through her sister's. "We're going to sing Christmas carols soon."

Iris smiled at her sister. "I'll join you in a minute."

Violet turned to give him an assessing look. Her eyes were a lighter shade of blue, but there could be no doubt that they were siblings. "Do you sing, my lord?"

He chuckled. "Rest assured, you do *not* want to hear me sing."

Violet took him at his word and went to join the small group that was gathering by the pianoforte.

Iris gave him an arch look. "Perhaps you should have some wassail to ease your fears of performing."

"There are many things at which I excel. Singing is not one of them."

Instead of pouting, she shrugged. "I should go."

He was surprised at the reluctance he felt at the idea of Iris leaving his side. "Will you join me again after?"

She considered the request. "I can't ignore

everyone else. If you'd like to speak privately, you should know that I like to break my fast early. It's usually fairly quiet in the breakfast room at that hour."

He nodded and watched her go. At least he'd be able to continue watching her as she sang. And he'd be able to speak to her tomorrow morning.

CHAPTER 7

othing would have prevented him from waking early and heading down to the breakfast room.

Iris had been correct—there were only a few people at that hour. Fortunately, he wouldn't have to wait to speak to her again. She was already seated at the table, along with her younger sister and Seaford's sister.

"Good morning," he said as he passed them on the way to the sideboard.

He could feel Iris's eyes on him, but he didn't turn around. And the trio's voices had lowered. He hoped that was because they were talking about him.

Iris wasn't sitting in the middle, thank goodness,

and the seat next to her was still empty when he returned with his filled plate to the table. He would take that as a good sign.

"You're up early, my lord. I would have thought you'd be the sort to lie abed until midday."

He took a sip of tea and met her eyes. Their gazes held for several seconds. He waged and lost an internal battle to combat his worst impulses. "Do you often imagine me in bed?"

Her eyes widened a fraction at his outrageous taunt, but in the end, she merely shook her head in exasperation. "I'll concede the point in this match to you."

He behaved himself for the rest of the meal. A few people wandered in but, fortunately, none of the people who had appointed themselves to making sure he behaved himself.

"So what are you planning to do this morning, my lord?" she said when she'd finished.

Violet and Clara had already wandered off, and for the moment, they were the only guests still seated. The footmen were refilling some of the trays, and he knew that others would be arriving.

"I'm not sure. What does one do so early at such an event when many of the guests are still sleeping? I'll admit I've never been on this side of such a situation before."

She laughed. "We entertain ourselves. I was heading to the library to find something to read."

She stood, and he did as well. "That sounds acceptable. Perhaps you can show me the way? In case I'm ever in need of reading material, of course."

"Of course," she said.

He saw the ghost of something flitter across her face, but she masked it quickly. They exited the breakfast room, and he fell into step beside her.

"The library is on the second floor. It is quite large. You'll have to tell me how it compares to yours." She stopped and turned to look at him. "You do have a library?"

Did she think him a barbarian who didn't read? "Of course. Several, in fact. I'm sure you would enjoy exploring all the nooks and crannies of the various libraries in my holdings."

He froze as soon as the words left his mouth. No woman who wasn't already a member of his family had visited any of his estates. Not even his town house in London. He liked to conduct his affairs away from his residences. So much easier to slip away when it was time to go.

If Iris thought his words strange, she didn't show it. And honestly, he was overreacting. It was an innocent statement. He was tying himself in knots over this young woman, and he didn't know why.

They said nothing further as they made their way upstairs. Fortunately, they only ran into two footmen along the way. The men didn't even glance their way. Thornton was a fool. His host should have assigned a footman to follow along behind him to ensure he behaved. Wentworth would never be so trusting.

They arrived at the room in question. It was large but nothing out of the ordinary. It certainly wouldn't compare with the library at his country seat.

He followed her into the room, and she didn't protest.

They were well away from the door when she slipped behind a bookshelf that divided the room. Curious, he followed.

He wasn't sure what he expected, probably that she was scampering up one of the ladders to reach a book on a high shelf. Instead, she was facing him, arms crossed.

He stopped opposite her and waited.

She licked her lower lip, and he was powerless to stop his gaze from settling briefly on her mouth. He'd wondered, of course, what it would be like to kiss Iris. He didn't actually believe he'd get that opportunity.

"I would like you to kiss me," she said.

It took him a moment to realize she'd actually spoken aloud and that his mind hadn't conjured this moment out of his frustrations. He hesitated another moment as he considered asking her whether he'd heard her correctly, but he hated that it would make him appear the callow youth.

He compromised by closing the space between them, making sure to move slowly so that she had ample opportunity to put a stop to what was about to happen. Because one thing was certain. If Iris wanted him to kiss her, he most definitely wasn't going to convince her that it wasn't a wise idea.

He was still operating under the assumption that his fixation on this woman rested in the unknown. Spending time in her presence hadn't convinced him that she was just like many other women. To the contrary, his curiosity about her had only increased.

But his recent attempts to forget her with other women had led to an ennui with the fairer sex that had frustrated him. Kissing Iris Rowland might end similarly—with him feeling a cold indifference.

He stopped when mere inches separated them. She tilted her face up to him, and he couldn't deny that a powerful sense of anticipation was already thrumming through his veins.

He reached for her chin at the same moment she placed her palms on his chest and leaned into him. She was shorter than him, and he bent to kiss her.

The first touch of his mouth on hers was light, so the zing that sped through him was unexpected. Her soft sigh followed by a small sound at the back of her throat set fire to his senses. He was powerless to stop himself from dragging her fully into his arms, but she came willingly, her arms wrapping around his neck as though she wanted to keep him with her forever.

Their kiss deepened, tongues warring with one another. Her movements were awkward at first, making it clear that she'd never kissed anyone before. He'd wondered, of course, if there had been any other men after he'd thwarted her meeting with Miller. It would be the height of hypocrisy to ask her, nor would he censure her if there had been another. But one thing was clear,

Iris hadn't expected to enjoy their embrace quite so much.

He forced himself to break the kiss, but he couldn't let her go. He gazed down at her upturned face. Her eyes were closed, her cheeks flushed, and a sense of possessiveness swept through him. He'd never felt this way before.

Shaken, he continued to stare at Iris as her mouth curled into a satisfied smile. Her eyes were unfocused when she finally opened them, and he swore he could see daydreams and fantasies flittering behind them.

"I'm no hero," he said, surprised at the rough timbre of his voice after only one kiss.

Her eyes sharpened, and they seemed to pierce through him as she studied his expression. Finally, she pulled away, and he dropped his arms with great reluctance.

"No, of course not. I would never confuse you for the hero of a fairy tale. So if that's what you're thinking, you can rest easy knowing that I have no illusions about you."

Her statement shouldn't have surprised him, and he had to laugh at himself. Did he really think he could fell this woman with just one kiss?

He locked his hands behind his back so he

wouldn't drag her into his arms again. Because in that moment, he wanted nothing more than to do just that.

"Did anything precipitate this request?"

She looked away, and he didn't think she was going to reply. Finally, she sighed and clasped her hands at her waist. He wanted to believe it was to keep from reaching for him again.

"Last night, after retiring, I had difficulty falling asleep."

They had that in common. Thoughts of going to Iris's room had plagued him for hours. "Thinking of me?"

Her exasperated sigh had him wanting to laugh. "Not at first, no. I was thinking of my brother-in-law. And Celia's husband."

He frowned. That was not what he wanted to hear. "What about them?"

"Watching the way they behaved with their wives. The two of them were so devoted. And the way they would hold hands, stand a little too close…"

Yes, he'd seen it as well. "They couldn't wait for the evening to end so they could make love."

Heat rose to her cheeks. "And then there was you."

He stilled, forcing himself to wait for her to continue. He couldn't risk scaring her away, not when they might not have another moment alone. It was a miracle someone hadn't already walked into the library.

"I find it difficult to believe you're here because you wanted to see me again."

He shouldn't be surprised she still had doubts. "I did."

She was examining him closely, weighing the truth of his words. "I thought Celia and Lily were daft for even thinking such a thing was possible, but then…"

Unable to hold back any longer, he reached for one of her hands and brought it up to his mouth. "But then…?" he prompted with a kiss to her palm.

"I saw that same look on your face whenever I glanced your way."

One corner of his mouth lifted into a satisfied smile. He enjoyed the way her eyes narrowed in response. "I've always found that the best way to let someone know you're thinking about them isn't to ignore them."

"And no doubt you've had plenty of experience when it comes to pursuing women."

She tugged at her hand, but he didn't release

it. Couldn't release it. Her words bothered him more than they should. Not because they weren't true—all the ton knew that they were. But because she thought that she was just one of many when she stood far above any woman he'd ever been with.

A slight frown creased her brow, but she stilled and waited for him to speak.

"You are not just another woman I'm pursuing."

She let out a soft laugh, and this time when she tugged at her hand, he released it. "I'm sure you've told every woman you've been with the same thing."

"No, Iris. I've never uttered those words."

She lifted one shoulder. "Perhaps not those words exactly—"

"No."

"But in some other way, you've made them feel special, as though you saw only them."

She was starting to turn away. He reached for her and she stopped. Several seconds of tense silence passed, and then she lifted her gaze to his again.

He didn't release her. He liked the feel of his hand on her waist, and she didn't press the matter.

From the way her pupils had dilated, he knew that she liked it as well.

"I've never said anything remotely similar to another woman. And I was careful to avoid anyone who might want more than a casual encounter."

That crease between her brows was back again. "But I want to marry one day. I want what Lily and Celia have."

"Yes, I know. Which is why I tried to forget you after that encounter."

She looked away. "I passed that woman on the path, the one you were meeting. And I stopped to see what would happen. I saw the way she threw herself into your arms."

Her voice was small, and he hated hearing it, hated seeing the way she was drawing in on herself. As if she was doubting that she'd ever be able to hold his attention.

Before that meeting, he would have said she was correct.

"But you didn't stay."

She shook her head. "I'd seen enough. I had no desire to witness whatever was going to happen next."

He caressed her chin with the thumb of his other hand, watching the way she shivered at his touch. He had no intention of allowing Iris to leave until they'd finished this conversation.

"Look at me."

She closed her eyes for a brief moment, then straightened to her full height and turned to look at him. He was cupping her chin now.

"I pried her away from me and sent her home. Alone."

Her eyes widened. "I don't understand. You were there to meet with her."

"Yes, but then I ran across another woman who was on the verge of making the biggest mistake of her life."

She grasped his wrist but didn't pull his hand away. "I don't understand. I was already gone. I offered no impediment to your tryst."

"No, but you were in my thoughts. I couldn't be with that woman when all I wanted to do was chase after you and drag you back into the gardens with me."

He held her stare, willing her to see the truth of his words. "I tried to forget you, but it seems that I don't want anyone but you."

She didn't take that as a compliment, proving once again that Iris was wise beyond her years. "For how long, my lord? Surely not forever."

He winced at the accusation. She was right to doubt him, especially since he hadn't come here to offer her that which she clearly wanted. "I'm going to be honest with you, Iris. If we're to have anything, you need to know what I'm feeling."

She licked her lips. "And what is that?"

He barked out a laugh. "I'm damned confused. I've never felt this way before."

"Never?"

"No."

A smile broke out over her face, and his suddenly foolish heart lightened at the sight.

"Then perhaps we should explore this new emotion."

He had both hands on her waist now and was drawing her closer. "That might not be wise."

"Perhaps not, but it will be so much fun." And then she leaned into him again and raised her face for another kiss.

CHAPTER 8

To Iris's dismay, Wentworth pulled out of their embrace far too soon. He released her and took a step back.

He ran a hand through his hair. "I am trying to remember that I need to be on my best behavior, but you are making it deuced difficult."

It wasn't wise, but she liked the fact that he seemed so confused. "And if I don't want you to be a gentleman?"

Now he had both hands in his hair as he spun away from her. Somehow she resisted the urge to throw herself into his arms as she waited for his response.

Finally, he dropped his arms, straightened, and turned to face her. "I'm going to leave now."

Horror washed over her, and he rushed to add, "Not the house party. I don't think anything could incite me to leave right now."

She frowned as another thought occurred to her. "Was it that bad? The kiss?" She had to look away. "I know you've been with many women. I'm sure I could improve with practice."

She hated how her voice sounded so small and uncertain, but her suspicion that he hadn't enjoyed her kisses was beyond embarrassing.

He reached for her, grasping her upper arms and bringing her close. But it wasn't close enough for her liking.

"Your kisses…" His voice was filled with emotion. "It was unexpected. Beyond anything I've ever experienced."

She had to ask. "In a good way or a bad way?"

"In the most terrifying of ways." One corner of his mouth quirked up when he saw her confusion. "In the best of ways. Which is why I need to leave this library now while I still can."

He didn't release her right away. They stood that way for some time, staring into each other's eyes while he held onto her arms.

"Make no mistake, Iris Rowland. I want you

more than I have ever wanted anyone. But I won't take advantage of you."

She released an impatient breath, annoyed with his insistence on keeping her at a distance. He'd sent her away once before, and she hated the thought of him doing so again. She was of age to be wed. He needn't be careful with her. "If memory serves, I'm the one who led you here and asked you to kiss me."

"Yes, and I want nothing more than to bring you to my chamber and have my way with you right now. But this isn't a decision to be made lightly, in the heat of the moment. If anything more is to happen between us, I need you to be certain."

She couldn't help but take heart at his words. A very large part of her wanted to beg him to do just that, but he was right. She wasn't thinking clearly right now. But would she ever be levelheaded when it came to this man?

She followed him out from behind the bookshelf and watched him cross the room and stride to the door. The door that was still open and through which anyone could have come in while they were kissing. Or talking about making love, for that matter.

She was grateful then that at least one of them still had the presence of mind to put a halt to their very inappropriate behavior before they were caught alone together.

He turned when he reached the entrance. "I will wait for a sign from you that you wish to proceed. But be very sure about your decision, Iris. Because once I start with you, I won't be able to stop."

He left, and Iris realized her heart was racing. Wentworth wanted her, and for some unfathomable reason, he was acting like a gentleman. But he was still a rogue, and she knew that it would take very little to convince him that she belonged in his bed.

It wouldn't lead to marriage of course, but she realized that she wanted him too. She didn't think she'd change her mind, but she would take the time to consider what she needed to do next.

Lily. Her sister had married a rogue. One that had spirited her away. Iris needed to speak to her sister and get her advice.

She was heading to her sister's room when she stopped. What if she and her husband were making love even now? Her face scrunched. She had no desire to walk in on any intimacies between Lily and Seaford.

She changed direction and made her way to her bedroom. She'd ask one of the staff to deliver a note asking Lily to come see her at her earliest convenience.

It wouldn't be soon enough.

CHAPTER 9

Wentworth waited what seemed an eternity for either Thornton or Seaford to come downstairs. He'd prefer to speak to Seaford, but if he had to, Thornton would also do.

He wanted to wait in the breakfast room but expected their wives would be with them. So he made his way to the billiard room.

It was blessedly empty. He set the table anyway in an attempt to distract himself. He didn't really need the practice, and if truth be told, the act didn't occupy his thoughts at all.

Iris had managed to embed herself under his very skin, and he was starting to suspect that he very much liked her there.

He'd just sunk the ball for what seemed like the

hundredth time when he realized he was no longer alone.

"We didn't expect to find you here so early. Did you even make it to bed last night?"

Thornton's words set his teeth on edge. Somehow he reined in the sharp retort that sprang to his lips and turned instead to put the cue stick back with the others.

When he turned, he was relieved to see that Seaford stood next to Thornton.

Seaford was examining him a little too closely, as though he could tell that Wentworth was on edge and why. "Would you like a little competition this time?"

"No. But I do need to speak to the two of you. Alone."

He moved to the door and turned the lock. When he turned back to face the pair, their expressions were carefully neutral.

Thornton spoke first. "You're bored. You needn't worry, we can make your excuses when you leave."

He clasped his hands together behind his back and braced himself for the men's reactions. "How did you know when you'd found the woman you wanted to marry?"

Seaford and Thornton exchanged glances. It was the former who asked, "Iris?"

Wentworth's calm was fast slipping away. "Yes, dammit." He jammed his hands into his coat pockets and began to pace. "I don't understand what's happening. I had a plan. Being trapped here, I was certain I'd soon come to realize I was mistaken about her. That she couldn't be nearly as interesting as I suspected. Certainly not fascinating enough to account for why my thoughts continue to circle back to our chance meeting." He stopped pacing and spun to face them. "It was a good plan."

Thornton raised a brow. "You can't get her out of your thoughts?"

Wentworth's lips twisted to the side. "No, dammit, and it's deuced inconvenient."

Seaford settled into a chair and steepled his hands at his waist. "When exactly did you meet her?"

Wentworth winced. "It was near the end of the season, during that last ball. I'd arranged to meet someone—no, not her!—in the gardens. I came across her instead."

Thornton tensed. "What happened?"

Wentworth scowled. "I didn't ravish her if that's what you're thinking. I don't need to force myself on maidens when I can have my fill of female company."

"So you what? Had a pleasant conversation with her?" Seaford's voice was surprisingly even.

"I warned her that it wasn't wise to make plans to meet someone alone in the gardens."

Thornton and Seaford looked at one another, and Wentworth all but growled. "Spare me your platitudes about my hypocrisy. I know very well the irony of what I was saying, which is why I felt it best to warn her about all the blackguards who walk among us. Men who would have no qualms taking things further than a foolish young woman searching for love would expect."

Silence descended for several seconds, and he realized he'd all but yelled that last statement. He who could find amusement in almost every situation and who never raised his voice. But just thinking about the harm that might have befallen Iris out in that garden had him wanting to tear out his hair.

It also begged a bigger question he hadn't wanted to consider: why did he care so much?

Seaford leaned forward. "I won't ask you what exactly happened out in that garden, but only because it's clear to everyone that Iris doesn't fear you. But tell me, what happened when Iris returned to the ball?"

Wentworth frowned. "This was right at the end of the season, so nothing happened."

Thornton crossed his arms over his chest and watched him in silence. It was deuced uncomfortable.

Seaford continued. "With your other paramours, why are you even here, Wentworth? I'm sure you have a mistress, and London is filled with widows right now who are trying to avoid their families."

Wentworth dropped into an armchair. "I dismissed her."

Thornton's eyes widened. "Your mistress? And what about the other women?"

He shook his head. "There haven't been any other women."

Seaford smirked. "I see the problem now. You're obsessed with thoughts of Iris."

Wentworth sprang to his feet again and began to pace. "I don't understand it. She's a mere chit of a girl. Why can't I stop thinking about her?"

Seaford's tone was serious now. "Tell me, did you keep your assignation that evening out in the gardens?"

Wentworth grimaced. "No. I sent her away."

"Why?" Seaford prodded.

"Because I couldn't stand it when she touched me. I allowed it at first, expecting she'd be able to erase all thoughts of Iris, but in the end I had to push her away."

Thornton settled into the chair Wentworth had abandoned. "And after that evening?"

Wentworth faced them. "It's a pattern that's been repeated with every other woman. After the first few, I stopped trying."

"But things are different with Iris," Seaford said.

Wentworth frowned. "Yes."

A hint of a smile touched Thornton's lips. "She's very beautiful."

"And intelligent," Seaford added.

"And witty, bewitching, damn bewildering…" Wentworth realized what he was saying. Where his thoughts were headed.

Seaford and Thornton shared another significant look. It was Seaford who spoke. "You love her."

Wentworth shook his head. "I can't. I'm incapable of such sentimentality."

Thornton leaned back in the chair and grinned

at him. "You're looking at two confirmed bachelors who didn't believe in love."

Wentworth leaned back against the billiard table and frowned. "I know I'll have to marry eventually, of course. Secure the line and all that."

Seaford laughed. "That's exactly what we thought as well. But then we found ourselves bewitched by the women who are now our wives."

Wentworth folded his arms over his chest and closed his eyes as he considered their words. His thoughts had been dancing perilously close to this conclusion, but every time he considered that he might *want* to marry Iris, he pushed the idea away as quickly as it came. But the thought of another man marrying her, touching her, and bedding her…

He swore aloud.

It seemed that this Christmas he'd be giving his mother her deepest desire. News that he would soon be marrying. Because it *was* going to happen soon.

He just had to convince Iris she wouldn't be making a big mistake in accepting his suit.

CHAPTER 10

After their all-too-brief kisses in the library that morning, the world seemed bright and new. Exciting.

Iris managed to speak to her sister, and that discussion had gone better than she'd thought. She'd expected Lily to warn her to stay away from a man like Wentworth. Instead, she'd urged Iris to continue with caution—and to trust her own instincts.

Lily's husband was proof that a rake could reform his ways and become a devoted husband, but Iris didn't expect lightning to strike twice. Wentworth wasn't going to fall in love with her, let alone want to marry her.

Still, she wanted to be with him. It wouldn't

take much for her to fall in love with him, and she expected they would only have these next few days together. Despite the logical part of her mind telling her that it would be safer to guard her heart, her intuition was telling her to enjoy whatever he was willing to share with her. She could deal with a bruised heart later.

Her decision made, she wanted nothing more than to speak to him again. Like yesterday, the women and men were kept apart for much of the day. She could tell that Celia and Lily were feeling much the same way as her and wanted nothing more than to suggest they sneak into the billiard room to see what the men were up to.

It wasn't as though they didn't know how to play, after all.

Finally, it was time to dress for dinner. But today Wentworth wasn't waiting for her outside her bedchamber. Despite what he'd said in the library, she was beginning to worry about whether he'd changed his mind.

And then she saw him waiting for her at the bottom of the stairs. She didn't try to hold back her smile. The time for pretense was behind her.

Wentworth bowed over her hand and led her to the drawing room, which was already filled with guests. There was no privacy, but Iris didn't mind. Because Wentworth was being attentive. If she didn't know better, she would have thought that he was courting her.

It was impossible to miss the glances that were cast their way throughout dinner. She could all but read their thoughts as everyone tried to decipher what was happening between her and Wentworth. He was attentive but frustratingly circumspect.

Like yesterday evening, they were able to snatch a few minutes together.

"I hope it snows tomorrow," Wentworth said when they were finally alone.

Or as alone as one could be in a room filled with people.

"Are you hoping we'll be snowed in, my lord? I didn't think you such a fan of house parties."

The low timbre of his voice raced along her nerve endings when he leaned a little closer. "I am when you're in attendance."

She searched his face, telling herself that she would be a fool to search for any sign of emotional attachment from this man.

Women were gathering again by the pianoforte, and Iris's heart was beginning to race. She'd be pulled into the group soon.

She took a deep breath and pitched her voice so that it was just above a whisper. "Come to my room later."

She'd surprised him. But there was no time to hear his reply because Violet stopped in front of them.

"The two of you can chat later. Come and join us, Iris." She started to turn but spun back, as though realizing that she'd just been rude. "Of course you're also welcome to join us, my lord. We could use more men."

Iris met his gaze. "Will you be joining us?"

He winced. "My singing voice hasn't improved since the last time you asked. As for the other, nothing could keep me away."

Iris floated through the rest of the night. After carols, several guests divided into groups to play whist, while a few of the other guests took turns on the pianoforte. Iris partnered with Wentworth against Lily and Seaford for a rubber of whist. She and Wentworth won only one of the three games, but they came close on the other two.

Finally, at long last, people started bidding each other good night. Nervousness warred with excitement within her as Wentworth did the same. He didn't touch her, and nothing in his expression was untoward, but surely that in itself was a sign that he hadn't changed his mind. He was being careful so no one would suspect the fact that he'd be visiting her bedchamber tonight.

One hour later, she was beginning to worry. She'd hurried her maid along, pretending that she was tired and looking forward to turning in. Then after the young woman had left, she'd begun to pace.

Then she'd sat down to read but found she couldn't concentrate on the words.

Had Wentworth changed his mind? Or perhaps he'd been waylaid by another. What if Lily had told Seaford what might happen tonight? Her brother-in-law might have issued a warning for Wentworth to stay away.

That wouldn't do. She'd just have to go to his bedroom instead.

She was on her feet and about to open her door when she realized she didn't know where Wentworth slept. Frowning, she began to pace. Wentworth had seen her leave her bedchamber that first evening, but Violet and Clara had been with her. He might not know whose room they were leaving. Even now, he could be waiting out in the hallway for her to appear.

She rushed to her door and swung it open. She looked first one way, then the other.

Disappointment crashed through her. The hallway was empty.

And then Wentworth materialized from the shadows.

She could only smile, anticipation surging, as she waited for him to enter the room. He was silent as he turned to lock the door.

And then she was in his arms, her body pressed against the door as he ravaged her mouth in a kiss that spoke of his own impatience.

They spent several minutes that way, wrapped up in each other as they kissed their fill. She threaded her fingers through his dark hair and reveled in the feel of him pressed against her, the hard length of his arousal pressing against her belly.

Finally, he lifted his head and gazed down at her, his eyes dark with desire.

"I thought you would never open this door. I was beginning to worry this was your sister's room." He cupped her chin and traced her lower lip with a thumb. "Are you sure you wish me to stay?"

Lily had told Iris that when it was time, she would know whether she should proceed. She searched inward for a hint of doubt and could find none. Only anticipation and a sense of certainty.

She nodded. "But I'm afraid I used up my store of bravery in issuing this invitation. You need to tell me what to do."

"I'm trying to convince myself that I'm not dreaming."

He seemed so earnest, but Iris couldn't understand why. Surely there wasn't a woman alive who'd be able to resist this man.

She cupped his cheek. "I can assure you that you're not dreaming."

She wound her fingers through his hair again, enjoying the feel of the short dark strands between her fingers, and urged his head down. And then he kissed her again.

Iris was determined not to worry about the future. They would have tonight, and perhaps tomorrow night if Wentworth wasn't disappointed. When it was time to leave, they'd go their separate ways.

She would be headed to Seaford and Lily's estate, where her family was joining them for Christmas. She hoped that Wentworth would head to his own estate so he could spend Christmas with his family. But she wouldn't ask him. If he was returning to London to seek out companionship with another woman, she didn't want to know about it.

Perhaps when the season began again in a few short months, she'd be ready to move past this man. Find someone who intrigued her even a fraction as much as he did. But until that day, she was going to embrace the brief time they had together.

"Iris."

Her name was a low growl, and it sent a shiver of longing through her. She wasn't just some woman he was spending the night with. He'd been obsessed with her, curious about her, and his need was obvious in that one harshly spoken word.

She realized that she didn't know his given name.

He trailed kisses along her jaw, then settled his mouth at the side of her throat. Desire pooled low in her belly, which shocked her. She'd seen Seaford kiss Lily in a similar fashion. Had her sister also experienced this sudden onslaught of need?

"Yes, Wentworth?" She was surprised by her husky tone.

When he raised his head to stare down at her, his brows were drawn together. "That won't do."

Her thoughts were addled, and she didn't understand what she'd done wrong. "My lord?"

His frown turned into a scowl. "That's even worse. My given name is Henry."

The admission surprised her. It seemed like such an ordinary name for such an extraordinary man. "Henry." She tried it out, but now it was her turn to frown. No, that didn't suit him. "Can I call you Harry?" That seemed more casual, not quite so formal. She could imagine a Harry doing unspeakable things to her. Henry, not so much.

His smile widened into a grin. "No one has ever called me that before."

She must have overstepped. "I apologize—"

He dropped a kiss onto her mouth. "I like it. It can be your special name for me."

This was verging into dangerous territory. She couldn't have a special name for him. She was just one woman among many.

She should protest. Tell him that he didn't have to pretend with her. That she'd come to terms with the fact that they'd only be together a short time after which they'd both move on with their regular lives. Him to new adventures and other women and her to a respectable marriage to someone who would never make her feel the same way he could.

Her thoughts scrambled when he swept her into his arms and crossed the room to the bed. Instead of dropping her onto it and doing wicked things to her, he settled her onto her feet next to it.

He stared down into her eyes for several seconds before speaking. "I'm going to be careful, but you should know there will be pain."

His concern touched her. "I know what to expect, but I fear you might find me lacking."

He gripped her chin. "Never."

CHAPTER 11

She didn't believe him. Which of course made her a wise young woman. But she'd learn soon enough that he was telling her the truth.

"Am I your first?" He suspected that he knew the answer already.

She nodded. "My sister said that there are things you can do to ensure I don't fall pregnant?"

A sudden image invaded his thoughts. Iris round with their child, smiling at him. The thought should terrify him, but he was beginning to realize that Thornton and Seaford just might be correct. His feelings for Iris went far beyond desire. He wanted forever with her.

He nodded by way of answer. He wanted to tell

her that it didn't matter since he would take care of her, but he wasn't sure she'd believe him. He'd never offered false promises to a woman, but she wouldn't know that.

He would worry later how to convince her there would never be another woman for him. But first he had to go about the business of ensuring Iris became so addicted to his touch she'd never want another.

He stepped back and began to disrobe. Her eyes were wide as she watched him remove his coat and waistcoat and drop them on the floor. Then he removed his cravat and shirt, tossing both garments onto the pile. His valet would lecture him tomorrow morning about taking better care with his clothing, but right now Wentworth couldn't stop.

He enjoyed the way her eyes were glued to his chest, her mouth slightly open. It pained him to move so slowly, but he had to be sure she wanted him as much as he wanted her. That she wouldn't change her mind.

So he stood there, bare to the waist, and waited to see what she would do.

She didn't disappoint him when she settled onto the bed and leaned back on her elbows. "You may continue," she said with a wave of one hand toward his trousers.

He laughed, charmed.

He unbuttoned the fall of his trousers, his gaze fixed on her. Her breath was coming a little faster now. He wanted to tease her, but he would do that another time. He was already harder than he'd ever been in his life, and he wasn't sure how long his patience would hold.

He removed the rest of his clothing, the weight of her gaze tracing over his skin like a caress.

"I can see now what all the fuss is about."

He frowned, hating that she'd heard others gossiping about him. He wasn't surprised, not really, but the thought bothered him more than it should. Right now, here in this bedchamber, it was just the two of them. He didn't want Iris to think about anyone else.

He waited for her to look her fill. When she finally met his amused gaze, she smiled. "You can hardly blame me for being curious."

He settled onto the edge of the bed, sitting close without touching her. "Perhaps you'd do me the honor of satisfying my own curiosity."

Heat flooded her face, but her hands rose to the

ribbon that was tied at the front of her chemise, holding it in place.

He waited, but it seemed Iris might have reached the limits of her bravado. His fingers met hers, and he pulled at the ribbon, his eyes fixed on the way the fine white fabric parted, revealing her breasts.

"I'm not well endowed—"

He stopped her protest with a hungry kiss. "You're perfect, Iris."

He allowed her to take the lead, enjoying the way her gaze, then her hands wandered over his shoulders and his chest. "You're so hard."

He pushed her chemise off her shoulders and cupped her breasts. "And you, my dear, are delightfully soft."

She fell onto her back, tugging him over her, and he went willingly. His mind was filled with everything he wanted to do with this woman. But somehow he needed to slow down, or it would be over far too soon and her only memory of her first coupling would be how much it had hurt.

He shifted lower and took one breast into his mouth, delighting in her taste and in the way she gasped and threaded her fingers through his hair. He spent some time there, going from one breast to the other, feeling the racing of her heart under his mouth and hands. But he wasn't a patient man, and his body was already threatening to spill. He'd already waited forever for Iris.

He trailed lower, kissing her belly as he tugged the chemise down below her hips. Somehow he kept from tearing the fabric as he shifted to the side and dragged it down her legs.

He rose up onto his arms then, looking down the length of her body. Iris bit her lower lip as she waited for him.

He hadn't thought it possible for a woman to take his breath away, but Iris did just that. And it wasn't because she was laid out in wanton abandon. No, he'd had his fill of women who were comfortable with their sexuality. But Iris's trust humbled him. He was her first, and God willing, he was going to be her last. The only man to see her this way.

"Do you trust me?" Her actions said that she did, but he needed to hear the words.

"Yes."

"Good girl. Now open your legs for me."

It took her a few seconds, but with a nod and a tremulous smile, she did just that.

And then he showed her just how he could

pleasure her without any pain. First with his fingers, and then with his mouth. He didn't think he'd ever be able to get enough of this woman. The way she gasped in shock, then moaned in pleasure.

And her whispered "Harry" when he covered her mound with his mouth had him almost spilling against the sheets.

It didn't take him long to bring her to her first release that way, and then he moved into place over her. She kissed him with abandon, not caring that he tasted of her.

He pushed into her, spearing into her with one quick thrust, and then stilled once her body gripped him.

He'd heard her gasp of pain, but they'd needed to move past that part quickly. He'd never taken a woman's maidenhead, and he was probably bungling the entire affair, but somehow he found the strength to hold still.

Her teeth had clamped down on the skin of his shoulder, and he wondered for a moment if she'd drawn blood. Given that he'd breached her like an inexperienced youth, he wasn't about to complain if she had.

Because the slight sting of her bite was nothing

compared to the bliss of being inside her. Mingled with the torture of not moving.

He kissed her, hoping to bring her back to pleasure. She tore her mouth from his after a few seconds and stared at him.

"You're so big."

He groaned and closed his eyes. This woman was trying to kill him.

"Does it still hurt?"

A small vee formed between her brows. "I don't think so."

He took a deep breath and summoned the willpower to draw out of her body slowly before easing back into her.

Her eyes closed, and her mouth dropped open.

He watched her carefully. "How about now?"

"Do that again."

He let out a relieved breath. "With pleasure, my lady."

And he made love to her then, moving in and out of her with care. Never before had he taken equal pleasure in watching the joy he wrung from his bed partner. Oh, he made sure they experienced pleasure—he wasn't that selfish—but their satisfaction had never served to intensify his own.

But with Iris… Each time she moaned and

clutched at him, the way her legs came up to embrace him… He felt as though his heart was going to explode.

Finally she came, and somehow he had the presence of mind to swallow her cries of pleasure with his kiss. When he pulled out of her to finish, he vowed that one day, soon, he wouldn't need to take such precautions. Because Iris was his.

He shifted onto his side, enjoying the way she came with him and settled into his embrace.

Her fingers traced over his back, his hip, and then she dropped a kiss onto his chest and looked up at him.

"Thank you, Harry. I hope…" She looked away, and he waited. Finally, after taking a deep breath, she met his gaze again. "When we leave here, I hope you think of me fondly from time to time."

He rolled over her again, caging her body under his as he stared into her eyes.

"I'm not even close to being done with you."

CHAPTER 12

*I*ris woke with a smile on her face. Last night had been glorious. Despite the fact they'd only made love once—she'd told him she was too sore to do so again—he'd spent most of the night with her.

He'd slipped out just before dawn, dropping a kiss onto her forehead before leaving.

She rolled over and buried her face in the pillow that still smelled like him. She couldn't name the scent, but it was now her favorite.

She'd been dreaming of him before she woke, and she closed her eyes, trying to recapture the final images. They were back in that garden where they'd met, and he was saying something to her…

Her eyes sprang open. He'd told her that he loved her in the dream. Even worse, she'd vowed that she would never love another man.

She sprang from the bed and stared down at the mussed sheets in horror.

She was in love with Wentworth.

She began to pace. This was terrible. They would only have one more night together, and then they'd both be leaving. Her to join her family in celebrating Christmas with Lily at Seaford's estate and him to London.

And other women.

No, this wouldn't do. She couldn't be in love with the man. She was behaving like any other sentimental young fool. Her emotions were all tangled up because Wentworth had been kind to her, passionate, and generous.

And no man would ever be able to compete.

She'd made a terrible mistake.

She sank down onto the bed again and reached for his pillow, hugging it to her chest. No, it hadn't been a mistake. Unwise, perhaps, but she didn't regret being with him.

But one thing was painfully clear—she couldn't spend another night with him. Her heart already ached with the knowledge she couldn't have him. If she allowed herself to spend another night with him, her heart would never recover.

CHAPTER 13

*I*ris was avoiding him, and he didn't know why.

After spending most of the day apart, she'd been distant with him over dinner. Cordial. Polite.

He hated it.

When the meal was over, he watched her leave the dining room with the other women. Then he rose and rounded the table. He approached Thornton, then Seaford, and inclined his head to one side of the room.

They weren't alone, but he no longer cared about discretion. If the others wanted to listen in on their conversation, they were welcome. "Iris is ignoring me," he said.

Thornton frowned. "What did you do?"

"Nothing!" He winced. He lowered his voice so it was barely above a whisper before adding, "We were together last night, but I swear upon my honor that it was consensual. *She* invited *me* to her bedchamber."

Seaford raised one brow. "And?"

"It was glorious. Incredible. The best night of my life. But now she's barely speaking to me, and I don't understand why."

Both men folded their arms across their chests as though they'd coordinated the movement. It was Seaford who spoke. "What are your intentions? Are you disappointed because you were hoping to spend another night with her before going on your merry way?"

Wentworth scowled. "No." He realized he'd spoken far too loudly when several heads turned in his direction. "Iris is mine. I want to marry her."

Thornton's eyes widened in surprise. Seaford, however, clapped him on the back. He didn't appear to be surprised by the outburst. "You left her satisfied?"

"Of course. I need to speak to her."

Thornton let out a resigned breath. "We can hardly allow you to spirit her away. But perhaps our wives can lure her away from the ballroom so you can speak to her."

Relief flooded through him. "Thank you. I am forever in your debt."

"Don't thank us yet," Seaford said. "The Rowland women can be quite stubborn."

They made him wait an interminable quarter of an hour before announcing it was time to join the women for the evening.

After entering the ballroom, Wentworth scanned the clusters of women. He found Iris sitting between two older women. She would have heard the men enter the room—several were arguing about whether they would wake up to snow tomorrow—but she didn't glance their way.

Iris was definitely pulling away from him, and he needed to find out why so he could fix the situation. If she were any other woman, he would have celebrated the fact that there would be no awkward displays, simply a mutual parting of the ways after an enjoyable night together. But Iris's distance left him feeling as though he were missing a part of himself.

He moved to one side of the room, careful to keep her within his sight lest she change her mind and give him a sign that she wanted him to approach her. But she concentrated on the two women sitting next to her to the exclusion of all else.

True to their word, Thornton and Seaford approached their wives. After a short conversation, during which both women glanced his way, Viscountess Thornton and the Countess of Seaford approached Iris and said something to her. Probably asked her to go with them since Iris rose and followed the women from the room.

She didn't look at him, but it was clear she knew exactly where he was standing. It was the one part of the room she avoided looking at.

Seaford approached. "They're taking her just down the hall. We'll stand by the door to delay anyone from leaving the room, but we won't be able to bar the exit for long."

The constriction around his heart was beginning to ease. "Thank you."

He slipped from the room and spotted the trio of women clustered down the hall a fair distance away. Iris was clutching her sister's hand and whispering something to her.

He started toward the group, his steps faltering when Iris turned to look at him. The pain on her face tore at him.

He inclined his head to the two women. "Thank you for understanding and agreeing to give us a moment to speak."

Seaford's wife frowned. "Have a care with my sister's heart."

He nodded.

Iris watched them go, the expression on her face forlorn.

Somehow he kept from reaching for her. "Are you angry with me? Did I fumble last night horribly?"

She met his gaze then. "No, Harry. You were wonderful."

He took heart from the fact that she wasn't insisting on formality between them. "So why are you ignoring me now?"

She folded her arms around her waist as though he was hurting her. "I'm falling in love with you."

Her admission left him stunned. He'd hoped for as much, but given the distance she was trying to erect between them, he feared he'd done something to make her hate him.

"Just so," she said, her voice shaky. As though she were trying to hold back tears. "It's a disaster. It seems that I am unable to conduct a short affair with you. I only ask that you respect my wishes and not press me further on this."

She wasn't making any sense. "Because you love me."

"Yes. And you don't engage in love affairs. Just physical ones."

One corner of his mouth lifted. "What if I decided that I could?"

She searched his eyes, looking for something. Whatever it was, she didn't find it, because she shook her head. "My heart would never survive. We can't continue on this path. If I'm to get past the inconvenient feelings I've developed for you, we need to end things now."

She brushed past him, and he watched her hurry down the hall. When she reached the entrance, she stopped and took a deep breath. Then, shoulders back and head held high, she entered the ballroom.

Iris loved him. But she was leaving because she needed to guard her heart.

He couldn't have that, so of course he followed. When he entered the room, she was standing with her cousin and sister again.

"Iris Rowland."

His voice rang out throughout the room, and

every eye turned to him. Everyone except Iris. She stiffened, but she didn't turn to look at him.

It seemed he was going to need to make a spectacle of himself. It was a good thing he didn't really care what everyone was thinking. He only cared about the woman he loved.

"Please look at me, Iris."

Some were starting to whisper, but they were quickly shushed. No one wanted to miss what was happening.

Iris turned, and he crossed the room to stand before her.

"I can't honor your request because, you see, I love you. And I want only you."

Iris's eyes widened in shock. Then she shook her head.

Determination coursed through him, and he dropped onto one knee. When he reached for her hand, she didn't resist.

"Iris Rowland, would you do me the honor of becoming my wife?"

She stared at him. "But…" She swallowed. "Are you certain?"

He scanned the other guests who'd now all moved closer to surround them in a tight circle.

When he met her gaze again, a look of wonder was starting to form on her face.

"It seems you bewitched me that night we met. Please put me out of my misery and say you'll marry me."

She was nodding now. "Yes, I will. Of course I will."

He rose to his feet and pulled her into his arms.

"I can't believe you made a public declaration," she murmured against his jaw before placing a soft kiss there. "You won't be able to take it back now."

He stared down at her, a feeling like nothing he'd ever experienced settling over him. Joy. Certainty.

Happiness.

"I guess that means you're stuck with me now." And then he kissed her because there was nothing like a public scandal to bind a woman to your side. Just in case she was beginning to have any second thoughts.

EPILOGUE

Christmas Eve

Wentworth had managed to convince Seaford to invite him to his estate to celebrate Christmas with his family and the Rowlands. It was actually a practical suggestion since Wentworth still had to ask Iris's father for permission to marry his daughter. Technically, he should have done that before proclaiming his love to a full room, but he'd been a little desperate.

He wasn't surprised that he and Iris weren't allowed to share his carriage. Still, he couldn't help his sullen mood when Seaford joined him, telling him that the women would enjoy chatting together in the other carriage.

But he'd had his revenge when the first flakes of snow started to fall when they reached the estate. He suspected Seaford had planned to ask him to leave after Christmas Day, but it seemed nature was on Wentworth's side.

Mr. Rowland's surprise that there would be another guest for Christmas had passed quickly. With a wry comment about how his daughters seemed to be making a habit of bringing gentlemen home for Christmas, he led Wentworth to the library. Rowland wasn't nearly as thorough in questioning him about his intentions as he should have been, but he did grant his permission for them to wed.

Everything seemed to be going his way. Except, as had been his lot in life since he first stumbled upon Iris out in that garden, it seemed he would have to wait even longer to claim her fully. Three weeks for the banns to be read in the parish church. Fortunately, his mother had written back to assure him that she would see to it that they were also read at the parish on his country seat.

All too soon, Iris would be returning home with her father and sister, and then Wentworth would have to wait those three weeks here at Seaford's estate. Because while Rowland might be pleased about his daughter's upcoming marriage, he clearly wasn't foolish enough to allow them to remain under the same roof for weeks on end.

Which meant they'd have to make the most of the little time they had together until they were separated.

Grateful for the note Iris had slipped into his hands with directions, he was able to steal into her room again that night. Everyone knew what was happening, but that didn't mean they shouldn't be discreet.

After making love, they lay together. Iris's head rested on his chest, and he ran a hand along her spine. A bone-deep contentment settled through him. After they married, he would have to ensure she slept in his bed every night.

Iris lifted her head then, a small frown on her face.

"What's the matter, love? Surely you're not already tired of our lovemaking."

Iris sighed. "I'm worried about Papa."

His hand stilled on her back. "Your father seems well. Happy, even."

"Yes, and that is most unusual. He doesn't come

to Viscount Thornton's house party because he finds it draining to be with so many people over several days."

He could understand that. Some people didn't like to socialize. "So why are you worried?"

"Because he was here when we arrived. The dowager countess invited him to spend time here while we were away… and he accepted! Last year he refused the invitation to spend Christmas Day here, but now here we all are. I think he might be lonely. Which makes me feel horrible for abandoning him."

He could imagine what had enticed Rowland to visit Seaford's mother while she was home alone. They were being circumspect, but he caught the way they seemed to light up when in each other's presence. And there had been a few significant glances when the older couple thought no one was looking. If the pair weren't yet lovers, they were well on their way.

If Wentworth wasn't mistaken, Seaford also knew what his mother was up to. But how much would Iris want to know? He had no proof, just supposition, and this wasn't his secret to tell. It was no one's business if the older couple wanted to spend time together. And he had no way of knowing just how far they'd gone when it came to comforting one another.

"You shouldn't feel guilty. Lily is already married, and soon you will be as well. Violet might find someone during this next season. It makes sense that he wants to spend time with a family who is near."

Iris's frown deepened. "If he becomes lonely, can we invite him to live with us?"

He started stroking his hand along her spine again, enjoying the way she leaned into his touch unselfconsciously. "Of course. But I think that your father likes it here."

Iris examined him, and he realized that he was on the verge of giving away Rowland's secret love affair. It was time to change the subject. "You need to speak to your cousin about next year's Christmas party. It is ridiculous how her mother-in-law insists on keeping the men and women separated all day."

Iris's brow smoothed. "I thought the men preferred that."

He rolled her onto her back and hovered over her. "This man certainly didn't. And I can guarantee that Thornton and Seaford didn't either."

Iris giggled. He loved hearing her laugh. "I take

it that means we'll be coming down next year for the Christmas house party?"

The things he did for love. But gazing down at the woman who would soon be his wife, he knew that he would spend a lifetime trying to make her happy.

The Baron's Return

Courting the Earl

Tempting the Viscount

Christmas Scandals series:

A Viscount for Christmas

A Highwayman for Christmas

A Rogue for Christmas

Hathaway Heirs series:

Lady Hathaway's Proposal

Lord Hathaway's Bride

Captain Hathaway's Dilemma

Miss Hathaway's Wish

For more information please visit the author's website:

suzannamedeiros.com/books

ABOUT SUZANNA

USA Today bestselling author Suzanna Medeiros was born and raised in Toronto, Canada. Her love for the written word led her to pursue a degree in English Literature from the University of Toronto. She went on to earn a Bachelor of Education degree but graduated at a time when no teaching jobs were available. After working at a number of interesting places, including a federal inquiry, a youth probation office, and the Office of the Fire Marshal of Ontario, she decided to pursue her first love—writing.

Suzanna is married to her own hero and is the proud mother of twin daughters. She is an avowed romantic who enjoys spending her days writing love stories.

She would like to thank her parents for showing her that love at first sight and happily ever after really do exist.

To learn about Suzanna Medeiros's future books (and to receive a bonus short story!) sign up for her newsletter:

suzannamedeiros.com/newsletter

Visit her website:

suzannamedeiros.com

Or visit her on Facebook:

facebook.com/AuthorSuzannaMedeiros

www.ingramcontent.com/pod-product-compliance
Lightning Source LLC
Chambersburg PA
CBHW061108310726
48974CB00002B/441